First published in Great Britain in 2015 by Comma Press.
www.commapress.co.uk
Copyright © in the name of the individual contributor.
This collection copyright © Comma Press 2015.

'Briar Road' by Jonathan Buckley © Jonathan Buckley 2015
'Bunny' by Mark Haddon © Mark Haddon 2015
'Do it Now, Jump the Table' by Jeremy Page © Jeremy Page 2015
'Broderie Anglaise' by Frances Leviston © Frances Leviston 2015
'The Assassination of Margaret Thatcher' by Hilary Mantel first published
in *The Assassination of Margaret Thatcher* © Hilary Mantel 2015.

This collection is entirely a work of fiction. The names, characters and
incidents portrayed in it are entirely the work of the authors' imagination.
Any resemblance to actual persons, living or dead, events, organisations or
localities, is entirely coincidental. The opinions of the authors are not
those of the publisher.

ISBN-13   9781905583799
ISBN-10   1905583799

The publisher gratefully acknowledges the assistance of
Literature Northwest and Arts Council England across all its projects.

Set in Bembo 11/13 by David Eckersall.
Printed and bound in England by CPI Group (UK) Ltd, Croydon, CR0 4YY ·

2015

THE BBC NATIONAL SHORT STORY AWARD

WITH BOOK TRUST

Contents

Introduction

'I TAKE SIX OR SEVEN years to write really small books,' wrote the novelist Mohsin Hamid. 'There is a kind of aesthetic of leanness, of brevity.' Hamid's books are worth the seven year wait. He's the author of *The Reluctant Fundamentalist* and *How to Get Filthy Rich in Rising Asia*, as well as a former judge of the BBC National Short Story Award. Leanness, brevity, precision of expression: I am attracted to these qualities in the art of story-telling because I have spent my working life telling stories on television and radio. Writing for the spoken word requires an economy, a stripping away of the fat, a paring back to what is essential. Each word must count. Each sentence must bear its own carefully determined burden.

That's why it was, for me, a joy to dive into this year's entries and to immerse myself in so many stories where the discipline of brevity was so evidently mastered and cherished. The short story can be read at a single sitting. 'It is a mystery to me that short stories are not being enjoyed in massive numbers,' said my fellow judge Ian Rankin, himself a master of the short story, 'since their form seems to fit our fast-moving world, a world of crisp emails and 140-character expositions.'

But it is not just brevity; concision matters too – the art of making the fewest words carry the greatest burden of narrative drive, tension, atmosphere, sentiment, emotion, wit, even humour. You can summon an entire world in 8,000 words or fewer, and the pointed brevity of your words will make it resonate in your reader's mind with a force that is out of all proportion to the slimness of the word-count.

It is ten years since the BBC and Book Trust inaugurated this Award. That was a time when the British short story was thought to be all but dead. Whatever has happened in the intervening decade, and perhaps with a little help from the Award's following wind, the short story has rebounded into robust health. Four hundred and forty entries were whittled down to a long list of 63 for the judges to consider, from which we chose this shortlist of five.

We chose them blind – reading the stories without knowing who the writers were. We didn't set out to choose an exclusively British shortlist, but that's what, by chance, we did. The stories gathered here are confidently rooted in British experience, and take us into corners of the country – emotional as well as physical – that are often overlooked.

The shortlisted authors are all accomplished in other forms: they are novelists, travel writers, in one case, a poet. It suggests the short story – ten years after the last rites were being read – is attracting a wider community of writers than ever. The churning, accumulated human hatred that Hilary Mantel's 'The Assassination of Margaret Thatcher' drops into an otherwise conventional middle-class English setting is profoundly disturbing and divisive. The prose is drinkably liquid and draws you into an enclosed world in which moral certainties are let slip and cast adrift.

There is a poetic quality to the prose in Frances Leviston's 'Broderie Anglaise'. The story has form and pace and careful disclosure, and uses what seems, superficially, a mundane domestic task to unpick the knotty tensions between family members – in this case, all women.

Mark Haddon's 'Bunny' gets off to a roaring, exuberant, excessive start and then quickly pulls us into the lives of two characters who are stunted and constrained by circumstance, but whose universal human yearnings we recognise. It is compassionate, original and darkly funny.

Jonathan Buckley's 'Briar Road' is a tightly-wrought close-up of a single moment in the life of a single family. The style is quiet, haunting, understated; key details are slowly revealed, hinted at rather than exposed, as tensions and suspicions accumulated over years emerge through the telling of the story. The human drama it evokes, the characters who people it, linger in your mind and demand a rereading – again and again.

In 'Do it Now, Jump the Table' by Jeremy Page, the story is lightly told. The prose has the quality of the spoken word and the dialogue is easy and natural. The story is almost casual in the unfolding. It is full of comic observation, but the laugh-out-loud funny moments are never far from the toe-curling error of judgment that the central character is about to make, at which point humour slips easily into something much darker.

I am grateful to my fellow judges; the generosity and quality of their scrutiny was an education for me. Di Speirs, the BBC Books Editor, has been the driving force behind this Award for more than a decade and does more than anybody to keep Radio 4 the powerful champion of the written word that it remains. The crime writer Ian Rankin, my fellow Edinburger and creator of the fictional detective John Rebus, is one of the Britain's most successful and admired authors. Sarah Hall is one of our most original and vividly lyrical young talents. It would take too long to list the prizes for which she has been shortlisted, and indeed won, except to say that she is a former winner of this one, and every bit as at home in the tight discipline of the short story as she is in the longer form. Tash Aw's debut novel, *The Harmony Silk Factory*, made him an overnight celebrity in his native Malaysia, and established him as a rising star in the UK, where he has lived since his teens. Thank you, my fellow judges, for the matchless intelligence of your deliberations, and the care you took to select the right winner.

Years ago, as a student, I handed in an essay without doing any of the required reading. I thought I could wing it. The tutor wrote one sentence on it that has stayed with me ever since: 'You have a pleasing turn of phrase but nothing much to say.' It was a rebuke I have carried with me all my life. Have something to say: no matter how elegant your prose, content is king. All our writers gathered here have something to say: about the marketplace of human affections in which we all trade – of the love and desire and hope, suspicion and fear and resentment, that are for sale there.

It is customary, when writing about the short story, to quote Mark Twain's well-known remark about short stories taking longer to write than long ones. I prefer something else the great American said: 'It is no wonder that truth is stranger than fiction. Fiction has to make sense.'

Stories – long or short – are how we make sense, how we interrogate ourselves, confront ourselves, and come to know ourselves. I have been thrilled to find the British short story in such good nick.

Allan Little

Briar Road

Jonathan Buckley

I HAVE THE ADDRESS, but it's not necessary to know the number. Briar Road is a street of sixty houses, and I could have found the right one blindfolded. It emits a frequency that cannot be heard but can be felt; it has the aura of evidence. Most of the houses in this street are in need of some repair: paintwork, gnawed by the sea winds, is falling away; window frames are rotting. The house to which I have been called, however, shows no damage. Every sill gleams like milk. Rashes of rust have broken out on many of the cars that are parked on the road, but the car that's parked on the drive here – a large German saloon – is showroom-immaculate, though far from new; the father's van, parked in front of it, is in similar condition. The edge of the grass, where it borders the little flowerbed, is as straight as a line of light. I have seen the father's business premises; other people in this part of town are struggling, but in this house there is money enough.

As was to be expected, it is the father who opens the door. The father was the one who read the statement to the press, and answered questions; the mother was in no state to talk. On television he looked like a man with whom you would not want to argue. In person he looks tougher: he is small and lean, and the rolled-up sleeves are tight on the disproportionate muscles; his gaze is confrontational and too steady; it would not surprise you to learn that he used to be a boxer. He has not shaved today; to the side of the chin, a complicated small scar is framed by the grey-flecked stubble. He looks at me as if I were selling something he would never want to buy, and is making it clear that he is not going to speak first. When I introduce myself, I manage four or five words before he interrupts. 'Come in,' he says, standing aside to let the intruder pass.

The atmosphere of the house is familiar: the air is becalmed; this is the stillness that follows calamity.

'Through there,' the father orders, jabbing a thumb. I step into the living room, where there is nobody. Every piece of furniture is aimed at the TV screen, which hangs on the chimneybreast, filling its whole width. Mitt-shaped armchairs, in caramel leather, flank a matching sofa. I am directed to one of them. Having dealt with me, the father steps back into the hallway and calls up the stairs for his wife. There is no need to do this. She knows I have arrived.

The seating is arranged symmetrically around a glass-topped coffee table, on which a newspaper is lying; there are no smears on the glass, and no dust; there's no dust on any surface. The glass figurines and photographs arrayed on the cabinet are regularly spaced; the pictures are all angled in the same direction. A faint fume of polish is in the air, and the carpet has been freshened. There have been visits from family, neighbours, sympathisers, police and other intruders, but it does not feel as though the room has been prepared for the benefit of visitors. My feeling is that the house is always neat and clean, but is even more so now, partly because housework, of course, is something that may offer respite from thought, and partly because it is important for the family to control whatever can be controlled. A form of sympathetic magic is at work, it occurs to me, as I examine the room. If everything is done correctly, the greater order will be restored, and their daughter will be returned. And to surrender to disorder, to even the slightest degree, would be to surrender absolutely, to the worst.

The father returns to the living room, and sits down in the other armchair. He leans forward to remove the newspaper from the coffee table; he sets it on the floor beside his chair. I note the tightness of his mouth, and the tension in the muscle at the hinge of his jaw. In such circumstances the father is under extreme and particular strain, because the father is always a suspect, as is the boyfriend, should there be a boyfriend, which in this case there is not, as far as anyone knows. If no boyfriend has been discovered by now, it's certain, almost, that there is no boyfriend. So the father is not immediately trusted, and for good reason. Weeping fathers have been proven to be liars, many times. This man has had to demonstrate his innocence. He has had to recount his actions on the day in question, hour by hour. Others have corroborated what he has said. But there is often a fault in such stories, a flaw that does not become apparent for some time. There will be people, still, who do not believe him, because it is often the father. This time, though, it is not. I know this.

He is looking over my shoulder, into the sky. Rasping a palm on a cheek, he makes a remark about a journalist – 'a snoop,' he calls her. It is to be understood that I am of the same company.

'They can go too far,' I sympathise. Then his wife comes into the room. She is more or less my age, the same age as her husband, but she looks a decade older; she moves as if using an invisible stick. Her smile is the smile of a woman who has come for a medical examination that may or may not reverse her prognosis. With something like deference she puts out a hand, which I enclose between mine. Her hand has no weight in it, no strength. It's like holding the body of a small bird, just killed. Her eyes are sore, and drowsy with despair.

'The boys aren't here yet,' she apologises. They are on their way, she assures me; in ten minutes they'll both be here. She suggests a cup of tea.

'Thank you,' I answer. One must never decline, no matter what one's preference.

Left to cope alone, the father can come up with nothing but the bluntest of questions. 'So is this what you do?' he asks. 'For a living, I mean.'

'Oh no,' I answer. 'I have a day job. In an office.'

'So this is a hobby,' he proposes.

'I wouldn't say a hobby, no,' I reply, and I smile, unoffended. It is essential in all cases that tension should be dissipated as it arises.

'How did you get into it?' he asks.

I tell him, briefly, how the faculty was revealed to me, when I was a young woman, when a relative was in crisis and I knew what was happening to her, although we were in different countries. It would not be appropriate, for now, to reveal that this relative was my twin, and that I could not save her.

'Woman's intuition,' the father comments.

'If you like.'

His gaze makes a detour onto my jacket, and he asks: 'Go to church, do you?' He thinks what I am wearing is my Sunday best.

'I don't,' I answer.

'Same here,' he says, in the tone of a player begrudgingly accepting a draw, as his wife brings in a tray.

A young woman accompanies her. She is twenty years old, I would say, and is six or seven months pregnant. Bad skin has been masked with expertly applied make-up; the eyelashes are heavy and the teeth perfect. She is bashful and nervous. This is the other daughter. She sits on the sofa beside her mother, and takes charge of the pot and the cups.

The mother asks about the Shoreham girl, but I cannot tell her much in addition to what she has already heard. Everything is fine between the Shoreham girl and her mother, I tell her, which is almost true. Confidentiality must be respected. The Shoreham girl is the case that has brought me here, by word of mouth. She went to a festival with friends, with the consent of her mother but against the wishes of her mother's husband, and did not return. The police were alerted but could find no trace. Appeals in the newspapers produced no worthwhile information. But I went to the house, and spent time in the girl's room, with the mother, and I could reassure her that no harm had befallen her daughter. In time she would hear from her; her daughter was in London, I told her, and was happy. And she was indeed living in London, and happy, with another young woman, which is something else I could have told the mother, who had come to me after hearing about the young man in Poole who had gone into town for the evening and vanished. He would be found living rough, in a town that had some significance for him, I had told his parents, and a year later he came home, having been sleeping on the streets, in Southampton, where a girl they had never heard about was living.

'He had forgotten who he was,' I explain. The Southampton story is an element of my *bona fides*, the summary of my successes. I make no great claim for myself. Some people can hear notes that others can't. Some tongues can distinguish gradations of flavour that elude the majority, some noses can detect a dozen elements in a perfume that to other people is a single scent. That's what it's like, as I tell them.

The father's attention is not focused on what I am saying. Several times, as I'm speaking, his gaze is directed narrowly at my mouth rather than my eyes. It has been said that my lips are the best feature of my face. And I have endeavoured also to make my voice pleasing. Its pitch, when I began, was a little higher, and the timbre more astringent. The father finds my voice agreeable, I can tell, though he is inclined to dislike me. But he would describe himself as a man who likes women, and as a man whom women tend to find attractive. This is obvious. Some years ago he was unfaithful, his eyes tell me, as does the glance that his wife gives him; he will be unfaithful again, I am sure.

'I can make no promises,' I say, presenting a frank face to the husband and to the wife in turn. I explain that it is not simply a question of opening a secret door and listening. Sometimes I cannot find the frequency. 'Every case is different,' I tell them. 'But I may be able to help you.' I have finished what has to be said.

The father has no questions; the mother has a question about the practicalities. A table is required, but the kitchen, it is agreed, would not be a sympathetic setting. The table will be brought through to the living room. Extra chairs have been borrowed from a neighbour, the mother tells me, as one would tell the doctor that one has fasted in preparation for the examination, as requested. A car stops outside. 'That'll be the boys,' she says, eager to start. She stands up, but it is not the sons' car.

'Could I see her room before we start?' I ask her.

The father needs to be told why this is necessary. It has to do with becoming attuned, I explain.

'I don't know what that means,' he responds, as if commenting on a remark made in a foreign language, by someone who is wasting his time. 'I'll get the chairs,' he says.

His wife leads me to the stairs and up to the daughter's bedroom. She opens the door gently, as if the girl may be asleep inside. 'This is it,' she says, in a whisper. Side by side, in the doorway, we look into the little room; there is a bunk bed, with a small desk below, and a chest of drawers, and an area of unoccupied carpet large enough for just one adult to lie within it. I take a step forward. 'I'll leave you,' she says, and the door silently closes on me.

A skirt lies under the desk, entangled with a pair of tights. The bed, unmade, has a magazine on it. Lipsticks and eye shadows are scattered on the chest of drawers. The police must have examined the laptop that's on the desk; they would have discovered the stuff that all girls hide from their families but disgorge to friends and pseudo-friends on the internet; none of it has been useful. Otherwise nothing seems to have been touched here. This is another aspect of the magic: there must be no interference with the attributes of the missing. To rearrange this room would be akin to giving up. So the room is as I need it to be.

I lie down, to absorb what the room contains. A huge birthday card, home made, is pinned open by the head of the bed. In the loop of the 6 of the big 16, two pretty faces are pressed cheek to cheek, blowing kisses. Other friends surround them, in a swarm of hearts and exclamations. All are girls. On a sheet of lined paper, LUV U is written in gold and crimson glitter. All around the mirror, boyish actors and singers smile at her. Amid the friends and the famous, the girl herself appears: on a beach, with her sister; on the back of a static horse; in school uniform; on a caramel-coloured sofa, between the brothers. And there's the one we know from the reports, the cute one, on a boat, wearing a beret. A soft pink horse stands on a shelf above the bed, beside a small Eiffel Tower.

This girl is guileless and much younger than the Shoreham girl, though not in years. 'Bubbly' is a word that has appeared in the papers, as it often does in such cases. There is certainly a great deal of jollity on show here, as there was not in the room in Shoreham. The pictures in the Shoreham room were postcards of old portraits; the books were indicative of thoughtfulness, of a more inward character than is evident here. Here I see no books of any kind. This is the room of a child. She has not escaped. The Shoreham girl had escaped and was alive, I sensed right away. And when the father – the stepfather – came home, and shook my hand, I knew beyond doubt that I was right, from the way his eyes shrank from me, and from the stain in his gaze, a stain that the wife could not see, it seemed. 'My princess,' he called the girl, and the word was putrid in his mouth.

In the room below me, a voice is grumbling; I cannot hear the voice of the mother. I close my eyes to summon the CCTV picture, the last image of their daughter. Leaving a shop, in a part of town in which she has no known friends, she raises her hood and steps out into the rain. I take into my body the air that only this room has. Underneath me, the father grumbles on. This is not a house like the Shoreham house. No love is left between these parents, but the situation is an ordinary one. Many children come through such things uninjured. Mine did. This girl was happy here. She has been loved. Silently, as if impelled not by myself, my lips form the words: *She has not run away*.

I hear a double slam of car doors, then a key in a lock downstairs. No sooner am I on my feet than the father knocks and, without waiting for a response, opens the door of the bedroom. 'Everyone's here,' he announces. 'You ready?'

'I am,' I answer, taking care to betray nothing.

As he ushers me out, his eyes perform a rapid search, looking for signs that the drawers have been opened and belongings disturbed.

The sons are awaiting me at the table. The older, his father's workmate, mid-twenties, in demeanour is a slightly softened version of his father, and clearly is attending under protest. I am something of a surprise to him — he had expected a fairground tarot-card act, and the woman instead looks like a lawyer. He takes note of the shoes, misappraising the expenditure they represent; his trainers would have cost more, I am certain. Like his father, he takes note of the figure too, but more blatantly, as if, by agreeing to participate in this nonsense, he has earned such entitlement. But the other son, two or three years his brother's junior, is a more personable young man, and is more willing to enter into the spirit of the thing. Apologising for the roughness of his hands, he offers a handshake; he is a mechanic, and the ingrained oil has made the ridges of his fingertips as clear as prints.

I have been given one of the borrowed chairs: its frame is gold metal, and the seat is a deep pad of red plush; the mother, to my left, has the chair that matches. The father is on my right, beside his daughter, who is next to the younger son.

In the light of the setting sun, the wall that I am facing is a block of radiant tangerine. It is too bright. 'Would it be possible to draw the curtains?' I ask.

The older son raises an eyebrow. The implication is that he suspects me of intending some sort of sleight of hand under the cover of semi-darkness.

'We must minimise the distractions,' I explain.

'I'm not going to be distracted,' he tells me. 'There's nothing going on outside,' he says, and he gestures in the direction of the street, inviting me to check for myself. His sister looks up into a corner of the ceiling; she is not close to her older brother.

'It will help me to concentrate,' I clarify, in a tone that might be taken for an apology.

By now the mother is at the window. For a few seconds she stands there, one hand on the drawstring of the curtain, looking out. Another day is closing. The evening is beautiful: the sea burning all the way to the horizon; a profusion of gorgeous clouds, dyed in so many colours. What she sees is an affront, I know. She sees the vastness of the sea and the sky, the countless rooftops, the traffic flowing away all the time, and it terrifies her; it feeds her grief. Her child is lost somewhere in this immensity, or perhaps is no longer in it.

I thank her, and extend a hand to ease her back into her place in the circle.

But the curtains are too thin. We are sitting not in darkness but in a burgundy-tinted half-light, like an artifical dawn. I become aware of the bright red dot that is glowing on the television set, and another on an amplifier in the alcove. I ask for the equipment to be unplugged, and for any phones to be turned off and taken to another room. Three phones are duly carried out. Then we can begin.

'We should join hands,' I say. The older son, of course, smirks at this. He makes his hand collide with his brother's like a small belligerent animal. 'This is what has to be done,' I tell the gathering, quietly. 'What we are performing is a ceremony, and this is the form that the ceremony takes.' The brothers settle their hands into a manly clasp.

When the circle has composed itself, I pause for a minute, directing my gaze downward; one by one, the five participants do the same. 'Now we should close our eyes,' I say. My voice is quieter now; the quality of the voice is important at all times, in any such ritual. It is theatrical, some might suggest, and this is not untrue, if a service in church is a piece of theatre. Mass is a performance, you could say, and by means of the performance the spirit descends.

I can tell that the older son is observing me, and the others, through slitted lids, but I do not challenge him; one must never do that. I keep my eyes closed and wait for him to join us.

'Now we must be silent,' I say, after a minute. 'I would like you to think of nothing.' I advise them as to how this might be done, and then we enter the interval of silence.

It is up to me to maintain the connection with the father: he has clenched his fingers into a rigid hook, which I must grip. But the mother's fingers are clamped onto mine like a padlock, and there is a quavering sound in her throat as she breathes. With a small motion of the wrist I rock our hands lightly, to calm her, to encourage; the quavering ceases, and her fingers yield.

Our breathing has become harmonious and hushed, like the breathing of tranquil sleepers. The circle is receptive, or as receptive as it is possible for this circle to be. 'I need you to picture her,' I tell them, when we have reached the moment. 'I need you to listen to her voice.'

Soon she appears. I see the girl rushing into the rain. She pulls up her hood and runs into the downpour, and disappears. Again and again she disappears. Then I see, vividly, a scarf – a gold scarf. From the reports in the papers I know that she was wearing a scarf of that colour. The scarf that I see is lying on grass. Slowly a landscape is clarifying: a hill, a low hill, no trees, some windblown bushes, an outcrop of boulders. This is a crime scene, but I am creating it. I do not see the dead, nor where they are. The dead are dead, and beyond reach. They do not speak to me and

I do not see them. My talent is not a special sight: it's something for which I do not have a name. When contact is made, a kind of shimmer runs through me, a presence as uncanny and as powerful and as fleeting as déjà vu. I cannot describe it.

The hill vanishes, and a new scene begins to manifest itself: a path, in woodland, and clothing strewn among undergrowth. The scarf is there, but it has no colour. A barn, a derelict barn, is surrounded by silver birches. This, I think, is a memory. I see a well, amid the birches; a sheet of corrugated iron lies over the shaft. It is a dreadful place: a memory of a place that frightened me many years ago, revived by the dread that has been seeping into me since the daughter's room. The girl is dead. That she will be found by a ruined barn, in woodland, is nothing more than a coincidence. Or perhaps a form of prediction, just as one could have predicted the arrest of a single man, aged 35 to 45, a man who 'kept himself to himself', a man with unhealthy predilections. I did not see her killer. And what I saw was something that I was imagining, I knew, and so I remained silent. I do not provide a commentary on everything that I experience in these situations. I exercise discernment. Possession is not what is happening, and I do not pretend otherwise, though many would prefer a performance of that kind.

'What's going on?' the older son interrupts.

I know that he is watching me again, but I continue without comment, without opening my eyes. The memory of the barn and the birch trees is fading, and still I have no sense of any presence. Out in the street, a man shouts; another man swears loudly from a passing car, and the first man, laughing, swears back. A single sharp snort is expelled by the older brother. It is becoming apparent that he did not care enough for the missing sister, and is troubled by the beginnings of guilt.

The woodland has gone now, and I am wholly conscious of myself, sitting in this room. I open my eyes, and propose that we change the structure of the circle. Under my direction, the daughter replaces her father, each son moves one seat along, the father takes the place on the left of his wife, but she stays with me. She takes her husband's hand, with a shake, as if urging a decisive effort, but they do not look at each other. This is the first time they have touched since I arrived at the house.

We prepare ourselves for another attempt. Silence is again achieved, but this silence has a quality of falsity, of simulation. It is not the true silence of submission. On one side, the mother's fingers contract on mine, as if she were a rock climber, fearful of slipping. On the other side, the daughter's hand is gentle. Her thumb strokes mine in a regular and unconscious rhythm. I glimpse the sisters together, laughing, but it's only a photograph put into motion. Now I see, at a party, someone who resembles the missing girl; she is with the friends from the pictures in her room. Sympathy is doing the work, but it's not sympathy with the missing girl – it's sympathy for the family. I want to help them.

By an effort of will I remove the pictures, but the involvement of the will is always an impediment. I am failing. Other faces emerge: I see the parents of the young man who had forgotten who he was, then the naïve and grateful face of the Shoreham mother. I see the Shoreham girl, the Folkestone girl, and the Colchester girl, who has never been found. So many faces appear, of the bereft and the abandoned and the hopeful. It is all interference, which cannot be overcome. I have to end it. Defeated, I come back into the room.

'I am sorry,' I say. 'Nothing is happening.'

All the hands unlink; I retain the mother's until last. 'What does that mean?' she asks, stricken.

If the girl were alive, I would know, if the circumstances were ideally conducive. But here they are far from ideal: there is too much resistance. 'I can't say,' I tell her. 'All we know for certain is that I haven't succeeded.' I apologise again.

'Should we try once more?' she asks me, but already her husband is pushing back his chair.

'I think the result would be the same,' I tell her.

The mother stays at the table, as all the others rise. As if it were a cavern of uncertain depth, she stares down into the tabletop.

Reaching into a pocket, the father says to me: 'So what do we owe you?'

'Nothing,' I tell him.

'We must give you something,' his wife says to me. 'For your time.'

'No, nothing,' I repeat.

The father does not press the point. 'I'll take you home,' he says to his daughter, as he pulls back the curtains.

In the hallway, the sons are putting on jackets, having returned their chairs to the kitchen. The younger one brings back his sister's phone; she has a hand over her eyes, and he places it beside her elbow, carefully. 'Thank you,' he says to me, giving me his hand; he will not meet my eye.

From the doorway his brother looks in; his gaze slides past me on its way to his parents. 'Call you later,' he says to them. Then, with a sniff of disgust he is gone, taking his brother with him. I see them striding down the drive, the younger lagging behind the older, whose walk has the determination of a man who is on his way to settle a score.

'Well,' says the father, looking at me; the tone of the word is interrogative and indifferent. His hands remain in his pockets.

All I can do is apologise again, which is what I do.

'Let's go,' he says to his daughter.

She picks up her phone and turns it back on, then offers me a brief and disappointed smile, as if coming to suspect that she has been deceived. She nods, and follows her father out.

The mother is still seated. 'Stay for a while,' she requests, touching my arm. If I leave now, the house will be empty and unbearable. I sit beside her, and she puts a hand, cupped, in front of me. I place my hand over hers. 'This wasn't his idea,' she says. I should not take offence at her husband's attitude.

'I don't,' I assure her. As a rule, I can see, the husband's ideas are the ones that prevail here.

'He's devastated,' she says. 'We all are.'

'You mustn't give up hope,' I tell her. 'Never give up hope.'

Undeceived, she says nothing, and the sentiment expires in the air. She regards the black rectangle of the television screen, but her eyes are seeing nothing.

'Shall we move the table?' I suggest.

It seems that she has not heard me, but then she answers, very quietly: 'We can do that later.' She looks at me, for five or six seconds, steadily. It is as if we have been talking about the situation and neither of us knows what is to be done. She releases my hand and turns to gaze at the window. It might be a picture that makes no sense to her; she has no interest in it anyway.

I move to look at the window too. Together we sit in silence for a minute or more, with our faces in the sallow evening light.

As if listening to the sentence of a judge, she nods her head. 'She was so lovely,' she says.

No words could be of use. No words are ever of any use. One can only attend. I place a hand on her arm.

When the tears begin, I offer her a handkerchief. She takes it, and presses it to her eyes with force, baring her teeth.

Sometimes love can be rekindled in suffering, but here the opposite will happen, I know. Men find it difficult to love, as women do not.

Her daughter was beautiful, I tell her. Whatever I say, I sound to myself like a priest who long ago lost his faith. But silence would be worse, I think.

'So many regrets,' she says. Her voice is a murmur; her eyes are riven by anguish.

I stand up to move my chair, so that I can face her squarely and take her hands in mine. We are joined, with her left hand in my right and her right in my left. There is no resistance now. If the daughter were alive, I would know it. Our hands are resting on my knees, as she talks about her daughter. She smiles and weeps, speaking softly.

Her gaze is fixed on our hands, as if they were instruments of devotion.

I will help her, she knows. When the violence of her grief has begun to abate, she will call on me, a year from now, or perhaps two, when the husband has gone. It is a mortal affliction and there is no cure for the pain of it. There can only be palliatives, of which love is the strongest, and she understands what I am offering.

Bunny

Mark Haddon

HE LOVED MARS BARS and Kit-Kats. He loved Double Deckers and Galaxy Caramels and Yorkies. He loved Reece's Pieces and Cadbury's Creme Eggs. He could eat a whole box of Quality Street in one sitting and had done so on several occasions, perhaps more than several. He loved white chocolate. He was not particularly keen on Maltesers, Wispas and Crunchies which were airy and insubstantial, though he wouldn't turn his nose up at any of them if they were on offer. He disliked boiled and gummy sweets. He loved chocolate digestives. He loved Oreos and chocolate Bourbons. He loved coconut macaroons and Scottish shortbread. He would never buy a cereal bar but a moist, chunky flapjack was one of the most irresistible foods on the planet.

He loved thick, sweet custard. He loved Frosties and Weetabix with several dessertspoons of sugar. He loved chunks of cheese broken from a block in the fridge, Red Leicester preferably or cheap, rubbery mozzarella. He loved Yazoo banana milk, the stuff you got from garages and service stations in squat plastic bottles with foil seals under chunky screw-tops. He could eat a litre tub of yoghurt if he added brown sugar or maple syrup.

He loved hot dogs and burgers, especially with tomato ketchup in a soft white bun thickly spread with butter. He loved battered cod and chips with salt and no vinegar. He loved roast chicken, he loved bacon, he loved steak. He loved every flavour of ice cream he had ever sampled – rum and raisin, Dime bar crunch, peanut butter, tiramisu…

At least he used to love these things. His eating was now largely mechanical and joyless. It was the sugar and the fat he needed, though it gave him little pleasure. More often than not it made the cravings worse. He hated people using the phrase 'comfort eating'. He had not been comfortable for a very long time, except sometimes in dreams where he ran and swam, and from which he sometimes woke up weeping.

He was twenty-eight years old and weighed thirty stone.

There was a creased and sun-bleached photograph of him at nine, standing in the corridor outside the Burnside flat wearing his new uniform for the first day at St Jude's. His mother had run back inside at the last minute to get the camera, as if she feared he might not be coming home again and wanted a memento, or a picture to give to the police. He was wearing grey flannel shorts and a sky blue Aertex shirt. He could still smell the damp, fungal carpet and hear the coo and clatter of the pigeons on the window ledge. He remembered how overweight he felt, even then. Whenever he looked at the photo, however, his first thought was what a beautiful boy he had been. So he stopped looking at the photo. He dared not tear it up for fear of invoking some terrible voodoo. Instead he asked one of his care assistants to put it on top of a cupboard where he couldn't reach it.

Three weeks before his tenth birthday his father disappeared overnight to live in Wrexham with a woman whose name Bunny was never allowed to know. At supper he was there, by breakfast he was gone. His mother was a different person afterwards, more brittle, less kind. Bunny believed that she blamed him for his father's departure. It seemed entirely possible. His father played cricket. As a young man he'd had a trial for Gloucestershire. He was very much not the parent of an overweight, unathletic child.

To Bunny's surprise he wasn't bullied at St Jude's. Mostly the other children ignored him, understanding perhaps that isolation was both the cruellest and the easiest punishment they could inflict. His friend Karl said, 'I'm sorry. I can only talk to you outside school.' Karl was a wedding photographer now and lived in Derby.

Bunny had kissed three girls. The first was drunk, the second, he learnt later, had lost a bet. The third, Emma Cullen, let him put his hand inside her knickers. He didn't wash it for a week.

But she was chubby and he was aroused and disgusted and utterly aware of his own hypocrisy and the tangle in his head when he was with her was more painful than the longing when he wasn't, so he cold-shouldered her until she walked away.

He scraped through a business diploma from the CFE then worked for five years as an assistant housing officer for the county council until he was no longer able to drive. His GP said, 'You are slowly killing yourself,' as if this had not occurred to Bunny before. He took a job in university admin, digitising paper records, but he was getting larger and increasingly unwell. He had a series of gallstones and two bouts of acute pancreatitis. He had his gall bladder removed but his weight made the operation more traumatic and the recovery harder than it should have been. Sitting was uncomfortable and standing made him feel faint, so he lay down at home and after four weeks of statutory sick pay he got a letter telling him not to return to work. His sister, Kate, said it was illegal and maybe she was right but he was tired and in pain and he felt increasingly vulnerable outside the house so he applied for Disability Living Allowance.

His sister said a lot of things that were meant to be helpful, over the phone from Jesmond mostly and very occasionally in person. She had married a man with a red Audi RS3 who owned three wine bars. They had two children and a spotless house which Bunny had seen only in pictures.

Bunny's few friends began to drift away. For a brief period his most frequent visitor was a bear of a man from the local Baptist church who was charming and funny until it became clear that Bunny was not going to see the light, at which point he too was gone.

Bunny had visited his mother every fortnight since he left home. She had always given the impression that it was she who was doing the favour, stepping off the merry-go-round of her busy life to make tea, feed him biscuits and chat. She worked in the Marie Curie shop and had an allotment. At fifty-seven she had started internet dating using a public terminal at the library and lightly dropped so many different names into the conversation that he didn't know whether she was promiscuous or picky or whether no-one stuck around after the second date. Despite the two miles between them she had come to his house over the past few years only when he was bedbound after his three visits to hospital. Now he couldn't keep her away. She collected his benefit and spent most of it on his weekly shop. She made him eat wholemeal bread and green beans and sardines. She said, 'I'm going to save your life.'

Once a week, using a walking frame, he made an expedition to the Londis at the end of the street where he bought a bag of sugar and a slab of butter. He left the butter out till it melted then mixed the two into a paste and ate it over three or four sittings. He would have done it every day if he had more money and cared less about what Mrs Khan and her son thought of him.

Bunny's paternal grandfather had been a policeman before the Second World War. He joined the 6th Armoured Division and was burnt to death in his Matilda ll tank during the run for Tunis in December, 1942. Bunny had a library of books and DVDs about the North Africa Campaign. He read biographies of Alexander and Auchinlek, Rommel and von Arnim. He made ferociously accurate military dioramas, sharing photos and tips and techniques with other enthusiasts around the world on military modelling forums: filters, pre-washing, pin-shading, Tamiya buff dust spray…

He watched porn sometimes. He didn't like images of lean men with big cocks which served only to make him acutely aware of his own body's shortcomings. He preferred pictures and videos of solitary women masturbating. He liked to imagine that he had found a hole in the wall of a shower cubicle or a dormitory.

He had thrush in the folds between his gut and his thighs. His joints were sore, which might or might not have been the beginnings of osteoporosis. His ankles were swollen by lymphedema. He had diabetes for which he took Metformin every morning. God alone knew what his blood pressure was. He ate Rennies steadily throughout the day to counteract his stomach reflux. Moving from room to room made him breathless. He had fallen badly climbing the stairs a while back, dislocating his knee and giving himself a black eye on the newel post, so he slept now on a fold-out sofa in what had previously been the dining room, and used the toilet beside the kitchen. Carers came to give him a bed bath twice a week.

Sometimes the kids on the estate threw stones at his windows or put dogshit through the letterbox. For a period of several weeks one of them with some kind of developmental problem stood with his face pressed to the glass. Bunny would shut the curtains and open them half an hour later only to find that the boy was still standing there.

He played Rome Total War and Halo online. He watched daytime television – *The Real Housewives of Orange County*, *Kojak*, *Homes Under the Hammer*… He spent a great deal of time simply looking out of the window. He couldn't see much – the backs of the houses on Erskine Close, mainly, and the top corner of next door's Carioca motorhome. But in between, on clear days, there was a triangle of moorland. If the weather was good he watched the shadows of cloud moving across the grass and gorse and heather and imagined that he was one of the buzzards who sometimes came off the hills and drifted over the edge of town.

On the mantelpiece there were photos of Kate's children, his niece and nephew, Debbie and Raylan, blonde, washed-out, borderline albino, in generic grey-blue cardboard frames with thin gold borders and fold-out stands at the back. He hadn't seen them in seven years and did not expect to see them again in a long time. Next to the photos was a small wooden donkey with two baskets of tiny oranges slung across its back, a memento of his only foreign holiday, in Puerto de Sóller, when he was nineteen.

Mostly he was tired. Hunger and disappointment were, in their own way, as painful as pancreatitis and he would have willingly swapped the former for the latter. And whilst his mother thought she could save his life, there were days when he wondered whether it was worth saving.

Then Leah came.

It was meant to be a temporary arrangement. She would live with her father until she got back on her feet and had sufficient money in the bank to feel safe. Gavin had pushed her out of the front door with nothing, not even her wallet. In Barclays she discovered that the joint account was overdrawn. Too ashamed to put in a reverse charge call home she spent the first night walking around the centre of Manchester, sitting at bus stops when she grew too tired to stand, kept awake by the fear that she would be preyed upon in some way. She rang her father the following morning but he took too long to arrange the money transfer. It was twenty-four hours before she could pick up her train fare from the building society, so she spent the second night in the women's hostel to which the police had directed her. It was not an experience she wanted to repeat.

Leaving the estate had been the first part of the grand plan. But you never did leave the estate, not really. You carried a little bit of it inside you wherever you went, something grubby and broken and windswept. You never trusted anyone who was kind. You married a man who made you feel ugly and weak and scared just like your mother once did, because deep down there was a comfort in being hurt in the old, familiar ways. So, in the end, the two miscarriages seemed almost a blessing, because they would have been Gavin's children, just like it had been Gavin's house and Gavin's car and Gavin's money. He would have let her do all the hard work then rolled up one day, lifted them out of the playpen and taken them away just like he'd done with everything else.

So here she was, working as a dental receptionist and returning each evening to the front room where she'd spent her childhood, sitting on the dove-grey leatherette sofa which stuck to the back of her legs in hot weather, filling the dishwasher in precisely the way her father said it had to be filled, having tea at six forty-five every day and never, ever moving the speakers off the masking tape rectangles on the carpet despite the fact that her father only played R & B and soul from the 60's and 70's which was music about dancing and sex and not giving a fuck about whether the mugs are on the top or the bottom rack of the dishwasher, because her father was coping with retirement and loneliness and ageing in the same way he had coped with her mother, in the same way he had coped with being a parent, by looking the other way and concentrating very hard on something of no importance whatsoever.

She met Bunny while scouring the neighbourhood for a strimmer. Her father's was broken and chores which took her out of the house were becoming increasingly attractive. She rang the doorbell twice because she could hear the television and after forty strimmerless houses it was becoming a challenge. She'd given up and was walking back down the path when the door opened behind her. 'Leah Curtis.' She was too shocked by the size and shape of him to hear what he was saying, the liquid waddle, the waist which touched both sides of the doorway. 'You were at St Jude's. You won't remember me.'

He was right. She had no memory whatsoever. 'You haven't got a strimmer, have you?'

'Come in.' He rotated then rocked from side to side as he made his way back towards the front room.

There was a yeasty, unwashed smell in the hallway so she left the front door open.

He bent his knees and rolled backwards onto a large, mustard-yellow sofa-bed. *Storage Hunters* was on the TV. The wallpaper must have gone up *circa* 1975, psychedelic bamboo shoots in red and orange, peeling a little at the edges. On the table beside the sofa was a tiny model battlefield – soldiers, sand dunes, an armoured car – and beside the battlefield, a neatly organised collection of paint tubs, aerosols, brushes, folded rags and scalpels, the tips of their blades pushed into corks.

'I get out of breath,' he said. 'Have a look in the utility room. Kitchen. Turn right. Bunny Wallis. I was in the year above.'

There was a garden chair, a bin liner of unwanted clothing and a broken bedside lamp. Maybe she did remember. 'Chubby Checker' they called him. She hadn't talked to him once in five years. She wondered if this was all their fault in some obscure way. She grabbed the orange cord snaking out from under the ironing board. She said she'd bring it back as soon as she'd finished.

'Whenever you want. I'm not leaving the country.'

She bought him four bottles of Black Sheep Ale as a thank you. Only when she was standing on the doorstep did she realise that it might not be medically appropriate but he just smiled and said, 'Don't tell my mother.'

'Does she live here?'

'It sometimes feels like that. Do you want a cup of tea?'

She said yes and was sent to make it. He remembered enough about her to be flattering – that she and Abby had run away to Sheffield, that she had a signed photograph of Shane McGowan – but not so much as to seem creepy. The milk was slightly off but he was good company. He gave her a Panzer captain from the Afrika Korps together with a magnifying glass so that she could see the details in the face.

She was going to say how much her father would like it, the neatness, the precision, but she didn't want to think of the two men as having anything in common, because in half an hour Bunny had asked more questions than her father had asked in two months.

He said his mother had put him on a penitential diet about which he could do nothing, so she came back a few days later with a box of chocolates. His doctor wouldn't be happy, perhaps, but it would make a change from the broccoli and the brussels sprouts.

When she was five years old, Leah's mother had taken her to the gravel pit to watch her drown Beauty's new kittens. It was a long walk and Leah cried the whole way, hearing them mewl and struggle inside the duffel bag. Her mother said it would toughen her up. She laughed as she held the bag underwater, not out loud but quietly to herself as if she were remembering a funny story. She wanted Leah to know what she was capable of. It was so much more efficient than hitting her. After that she could make Leah feel sick inside just by narrowing her eyes.

When they had guests her mother called her 'Darling'. So how could Leah tell anyone? It was fathers who abused their children. Cruel mothers were the stuff of fairytales.

Bunny didn't find her attractive at first. She was oddly shapeless, a skinny girl carrying too much weight. Her hair was flat and there was something sour about the expression into which her face fell when she didn't think she was being watched. But she woke something which had been going slowly to sleep inside him over the past couple of years. He pictured her naked, moving through the house, perched on the armchair, wiping herself on the toilet, standing at the sink. He could no longer get an erection let alone masturbate so there was no relief from these images and every fantasy left a small bruise on his heart. She was kind and bought him sweet, sticky things. They never talked about his weight and she understood the tyranny of mothers. Five minutes into their second meeting he realised how badly he needed her to keep coming.

The first carer Leah met was a pinched Polish woman who didn't offer her name and acted as if Leah were not in the room. She treated Bunny like a recalcitrant child with whom she'd been saddled for half an hour. Leah could see him flinching as she dried his hair. The second, Deolinda, was a big woman from Zimbabwe who kept up a steady stream of stories about the latest episode of *Masterchef*, about her uncle who had been tortured by the police back home, about the proposed landfill site in Totton… Then they were replaced by two different carers who were quickly replaced in their turn, and Leah could see that Bunny would prefer someone dour and ill-tempered if only they stuck around and knew where the shampoo was kept, took care of the models and made him a mug of sugary tea without being asked.

Her father went to The Wainwright and drank a half of Guinness three nights a week. Her father played The Blackbyrds and The Contours. Her father wore a green v-necked sweater or a red v-necked sweater. Her father smoked thirty cigarettes a day standing under the little awning outside the back door. Her father put the big plates on the right and the smaller side plates on the left and insisted that all knives pointed downwards in the cutlery basket. Her father recorded TV travel programmes and watched them at convenient times: the Great Wall of China, the Atacama desert, the Everglades.

She hadn't hated him when she was little. If anything she had thought of him as an elder sibling who was keeping a low profile for the same reasons she was. But now, looking back? How could you turn away from your own child? She said, 'You never stuck up for me'.

Her father said, 'Your mother was a difficult and troubled woman.'

She said, 'That's not the point.'

Her father said, 'I think something went wrong after you were born.'

She said. 'That's not the point, either.'

He never understood that she was asking for an apology. Or perhaps he understood but didn't feel an apology was appropriate. Either way, if you had to ask then it counted for nothing.

One morning Bunny's mother crouched on the far side of his bed and retrieved a crackly, transparent punnet which had once contained twenty Tesco mini flapjack bites and which Leah must have forgotten to remove the night before. 'What in God's name is this?'

He said, 'I've got a friend.'

She said, 'Do you know how hard I try to keep you healthy?'

After washing up and hoovering she returned to the living room and said, 'Who?'

He said nothing. He had leverage for once and wanted to savour it briefly.

'Well?'

'I used to go to school with her.'

'What's her name?'

He was surprised by how upset his mother was, and worried that she might go to Leah's house and confront her.

'How often does she come round?'

'Now and then.'

'Every week?'

'I have a friend, that's all. She brought me some biscuits. There's no reason to be upset.'

She punished him by not coming round for five days but found, on her return, that Leah had done the housework in her absence. She had also marked her territory by leaving four crumpled Cadbury's Fruit and Nut wrappers on the draining board.

She should have gone to London with Abby and Nisha and Sam straight after college. She'd be living in a flat in Haringey now, taking the Piccadilly Line to an office in Faringdon or Bank, winding down on a Friday evening with Jagermeister and chicken tikka skewers in the Jamaica Wine House. She might be married to someone halfway human. She might have children.

There was jubilation on Facebook when she confessed that her marriage was over, perhaps a little more jubilation than she wanted. She didn't go into detail. Nisha said, 'Get your arse down here. You are going to die in that place.'

Why didn't she pack her bags? Was she dead already? Did the memory of that close-knit foursome at school seem less rosy now that there was a real possibility of her joining them? Or was it Bunny? He was funny, he was kind, he was grateful. For the first time in her life she had someone who needed her, and she couldn't imagine sitting by the boating lake in Ally Pally or walking down Shaftesbury Avenue knowing she'd abandoned him to a life that was shrinking rapidly to a single room four hundred miles away.

Bunny liked her to read the paper out loud. He liked to beat her at chess and lose to her at Monopoly. They watched DVDs she picked up from the bargain box in Blockbuster. Often she would bring a cake, take a small piece for herself and make no comment as he worked his way through the rest. Sometimes she would go into the back garden to smoke and come back ten minutes later smelling of cigarettes. He yearned for her to lean over one day and push her dirty tongue into his mouth. Could you ask someone to do that kind of thing? Just as a favour? Because the thought of never being kissed again tore open a hole in his chest.

One evening when they were watching a documentary about Bletchley Park, Bunny's mother let herself in. She called out a casual hello, hung up her coat, came into the living room and said, 'So we meet at last,' as if this were a surprise. 'I don't think Bunny has ever told me your name.'

'Leah.' She didn't hold out her hand.

The two women swapped pleasantries for a couple of scratchy minutes then his mother said, 'You bring him biscuits.'

'Sometimes,' said Leah.

'You know you're killing him.'

'They're just biscuits.'

'I've looked after my son for nearly thirty years.'

'You don't like me coming here, do you?' said Leah. 'You want him all to yourself.'

His mother straightened her back. 'I just don't want him spending his time with someone like you.'

Bunny knew he should intervene but he was not in the habit of telling either of them what they should or should not do, and in truth he was flattered to find himself being fought over.

'Someone like me?' said Leah. 'What does that mean, precisely?'

Bunny had imagined this argument many times. He had always wanted Leah to win, but now that it was happening he wondered if his mother might be right after all. Leah was not his wife, not his girlfriend, not a part of his family. She could abandon him tomorrow.

His mother stepped close to Leah and said, quietly, 'You little bitch. I've got your number.'

On the table beside the sofa there was a diorama of five British soldiers surrounding a crashed Messerschmitt, the dead pilot slumped forward in the smashed cockpit. Bunny had spent five weeks making it. His mother swept it off the table and walked out of the house, slamming the door behind her.

It was the end of summer, but instead of cool winds and rainy days a thick grey cloud settled over the town so that the air felt tepid and secondhand. Two children at the end of the street were killed by a police car chasing a stolen van. Nasir Iqbal and Javed Burrows. The rear wheels lost traction on the bend and the vehicle mounted the pavement knocking over a brick wall behind which the two boys were playing cricket. He knew their names because they were painted on the street in big white letters. The driver of the car and his colleague were spirited away before the family and neighbours fully understood what had happened. The next police officers at the scene were greeted by a volley of stones and glass bottles and one of their cars was rolled onto its roof.

There was a small riot every evening for a fortnight. Through the curtains, Bunny saw the blue lights of police vans and heard whoops and explosions which sounded to him more like people celebrating a victory than mourning a loss.

He decided for the time being he wouldn't leave the house. He did not want to find himself surrounded by an angry crowd in search of an easy target. But when the streets finally became calm once more he found that he was still afraid. He told himself he would go out when he felt stronger, but even as he was telling himself this he knew that it wasn't true.

She got back from work one Wednesday evening to find her father sitting at the dining table with his palms flat on the placemat in front of him as if he were engaged in a one-man seance. He was wearing his red v-neck jumper. He looked directly at her and said, 'My trouble.'

'Your what?' said Leah.

'My trouble leg,' he said, slurring his words.

She assumed that he was drunk but when she came closer she could see that the left hand side of his face was sagging. She tried helping him to the sofa so that he could lie down but he couldn't hold his own weight and she had to hoist him back onto the chair. He was unable to say how long he had been in this state.

The ambulance took twenty-five minutes to arrive. Her father seemed completely untroubled by the gravity of the situation. The paramedic slipped a line into the crook of his arm and held it down with a fat crucifix of white tape. The siren was on the whole way, a dreamy mismatch between the antiseptic calm and the speed with which they sliced through the world.

When they arrived at the hospital her father was partially blind and there were many words he could no longer say, Leah's name being one of them. It was the length of time he had spent sitting at the table, so the doctor said. However long that was. After the golden hour the odds went through the floor. Leah wondered if he had realised that he was being offered a neat, uncomplicated exit and had decided to take it, because God forbid that he should ever find himself bedbound, or incontinent, or needing to be fed by someone else.

He had the second stroke just after midnight.

She sat in the hard glare of the relatives' room looking at a shitty painting of a fishing boat and a lighthouse. It was the lack of justice which hurt most, the way his cowardice turned out to have been such a good game plan, the possibility that he had never suffered.

She took a taxi back to the house but couldn't sleep, repeatedly dropping off then crashing back into wakefulness convinced that her mother was in the room.

She rang in sick the following morning and went round to Bunny's house. She wasn't sure he understood but he held her while she cried and that was enough. She told him about the kittens. She told him how her mother had called her 'a mistake' and 'a disappointment'. She told him how her mother had made balls of lard and peanuts and hung them from strings outside the dining room window in the winter for chaffinches and coal tits and robins. She told him how quickly the MS had progressed, how she wasn't allowed into her mother's bedroom during the final months, how her mother died and how Leah kept forgetting this because nothing in the house had changed.

Bunny said, 'I hate my father. I haven't seen him for twenty years. I have no idea what he looks like. But every time there's a crowd on TV I find myself scanning the faces, looking for him.'

She told him that she had trouble sleeping. He said she could move in upstairs if she wanted, and tried very hard not to show how pleased he was when she accepted the offer.

She put her things in Bunny's old bedroom. He hadn't been upstairs for a long time. The rusted hot tap in the sink no longer turned and there was velvety, green fungus in the corners of the bathroom window. On the dusty sill sat a pair of rusty nail clippers, a dog-eared box of sticking plasters and a little brown tub of Diazepam tablets with a water-blurred label.

The first night she drank whisky in warm milk to get herself to sleep but was woken several hours later by Bunny's snoring. She lay motionless in the half-dark. The gaps between his snores were growing longer and she could tell that something was not right. She went downstairs and pushed the living room door open. Bunny now slept on an adjustable bed which had replaced the yellow sofa-bed. The smell was rank and cloistered. She drew the curtain back and opened the smaller window.

He was lying on his back, his skin freakishly white, his arms swimming as if he were underwater and struggling to reach the surface. His breathing stopped for three, four, five seconds then restarted like an old motor. She wondered if she should do something. His breathing stopped again. And started. And stopped. Suddenly he was awake, wide-eyed and fighting for breath.

'Bunny?' She took his hand. 'It's Leah. I'm here.'

It was the fat around his throat, the doctor said, the sheer weight of his chest, the weakness of his muscles. If he carried on sleeping on his back he would suffocate. He had to remain propped up twenty-four hours a day.

Towards the end of the second week she returned from work to find that he had soiled himself. That morning's carer had not turned up and he could hold on no longer. She smelt it as soon as she came in. She considered quietly reclosing the door and going back to her father's empty house. Then Bunny called out, 'Leah?'

She stepped into the living room.

He said, 'I'm so sorry.'

She filled a plastic bowl with hot water. Soap, flannels, toilet rolls, a towel from upstairs. She helped Bunny roll onto his side. His flesh was raw and spotty and covered in large port-wine blotches. Some of the shit was on the sheet, some of it was wedged into the crack between his buttocks. She used wads of toilet paper to scrape most of it off, dumping the shit and the used paper in a plastic bag. She unhooked the corners of the cotton sheet and the plastic mattress protector beneath it and bunched them up, using the material to wipe him clean as she did so. She put the sheet in the washing machine and the protector into a second plastic bag.

It wasn't as bad as she had expected. This was what she would have done for her children if life had turned out differently.

She dipped the flannels in the soapy water and wiped him, lifting the flesh to get into the folds. She towelled him dry and left him to lie on his side exposed to the air for a while. She put the flannels and the towel into the washing machine with the sheet. She bleached the plastic bowl. She remade the bed with a clean sheet and a new mattress protector from the cupboard in the kitchen. She dusted him with anti-fungal powder then let him roll back into his usual position.

He said, 'You are the kindest person I have ever met.'

She found a letter from the council lying on her father's doormat saying that the tenancy had come to an end with her father's death and unless representations were made, the house would have to be vacated by the end of the month.

She took the records to the Oxfam shop in town. 'Higher and Higher' by Jackie Wilson, 'Up, Up and Away' by The Fifth Dimension, 'Nothing Can Stop Me' by Gene Chandler… She brought a small cardboard box home from the Co-op and filled it with the only possessions that seemed worth keeping, objects she remembered from her childhood, mostly – an owl made of yellow glass, a box of tarnished apostle spoons on faded purple plush, a decorative wall-plate with a view of Robin Hood's Bay. She locked the door and posted the keys through the letterbox. She stowed the cardboard box under the bed at Bunny's house.

It was a Friday after work. She'd just come out of Boots and was passing Kenyons en route to the bus station. The two women were sitting at a table in the window. She could see immediately that they were from out of town; the way they held themselves, the way they owned the space around them. The woman facing her had sunglasses pushed up into an auburn crop, tanned shoulders and a canary yellow dress to show them off. Leah felt a little stab of something between envy and affront. The woman caught her eye. Leah walked away in embarrassment and five steps further down the street realised that she had been looking at Abby and Nisha. She was about to break into a run when Nisha emerged from the doors of the restaurant. She blocked Leah's path, looked her up and down theatrically and said, 'What the fuck happened to you, girl?'

Leah had forgotten how it worked, the spiky repartee that bound them together and kept outsiders away. She looked down at her grey tights and elderly trainers. 'I've just come from work.'

'Inside,' said Nisha, nodding towards the door of the restaurant as if it were a cell Leah was being returned to.

The two of them were back for Abby's brother's wedding. 'Number Four. I can't even remember her name. Albanian? Slovenian? She looks like those pictures in the papers of women who've killed their kids.' Abby and Vince were now living in Muswell Hill. 'The Great White Highlands.' And Sam was pregnant for a second time. 'Ten months. He practically fucked her in the delivery suite.'

The waiter materialised with his little flip-pad. Leah tried to make her excuses but Abby held her eye. 'I don't know what you've got planned for this evening but I know for a fact that it will be shit compared to this.'

She ate grilled tuna with a salad of cannellini beans, roasted red peppers, olives, anchovies and rocket followed by lemon tart and crème fraîche. They drank two bottles of Montepulciano d'Abruzzo between them. A bill for a hundred and ten pounds and a fifteen pound tip. They smoked in the little garden at the back, next to one of the patio heaters.

'How's your Dad?' asked Nisha.

'He died,' said Leah, putting her fist against her mouth because she couldn't say any more without crying.

Nisha looked at her long and hard. No condolence, no consolation. 'We've got a sofa-bed. If you haven't found a job and a room in a shared house by the end of the month I'll stick you on the bus back up here.'

'I'm sorry,' said Leah. 'I can't do it.'

Nisha shrugged. 'It's your funeral'.

Two of the toes on Bunny's left foot went black. They kept the window open all day because of the smell. There was nothing to be done, the doctor said. Leah should keep them tightly bandaged until they fell off, then wash the wounds in salt water twice a day until they healed. Ten days later she found them in the bed while Bunny was sleeping.

She flicked them onto a newspaper as if they were dead bees, carried them outside and dropped them into the bin.

A fine, spitty rain was coming in off the hills. There was no-one around. A wing mirror hung off a battered brown Honda. The names of the dead boys were still readable on the tarmac. At her feet grass was forcing its way up through cracks in the concrete. If everyone abandoned these streets she wondered how long it would take for the forest to take them back, roots and creepers bringing the walls down piece by piece, wolves moving through the ruins.

She was crying and she didn't know whether it was for herself or for Bunny.

He knew that something was wrong. She was making an effort to be cheerful, to be attentive, to be patient. He had known all along that it would come to this. If he were braver he would let her go. She'd given him more happiness than he'd expected to get from anyone. But he had never been brave. And he couldn't bring himself to have one day less of her company.

He couldn't take his eyes off her. Now that she was about to be taken away she had become unutterably beautiful. He finally understood the songs: the sweetness, the hurt, the cost of it all. He would be wiser next time. It was just a shame there wouldn't be a next time.

She went to Sainsbury's and bought a chicken jalfrezi and pilau rice, a king prawn masala and some oven chips. She bought two tins of treacle pudding, two tubs of Taste the Difference vanilla custard and a bottle of Jacob's Creek Cool Harvest shiraz rosé.

He saw her negotiating the hallway with three bags. 'You bought the shop.'

'I'm cooking you a posh supper.'

'Why?' asked Bunny. 'Not that I'm complaining.'

'Big occasion,' said Leah.

'What big occasion?'

She could hear the anxiety in his voice. She put the bags down and stuck her head round the door of the living room. 'Trust me.' She turned the oven on and poured him a glass of the rosé. 'I would never do anything to hurt you.' She kissed his forehead.

While everything was cooking she lit two candles and turned the lights down. She carefully moved Bunny's models off the table and put them out of harm's way. Then she fetched a chair from the dining room so that she could sit and eat beside him. She laid the cutlery out and gave Bunny two of the chequered green serviettes to cover his lap. She bought the dishes in one by one, the prawn masala, the chicken, the chips, the rice. She sat down and held up her glass. 'Cheers.'

He said, 'I know you're leaving, and I know you're trying to be kind about it.'

'I'm not leaving.'

'Really?' He spoke very quietly, as if her decision were a house of cards which might collapse at any minute.

'Really.' She took a sip of the rosé. It was slightly warm. She should have put it in the freezer for ten minutes.

'Wow.' He lay back against his pillows and exhaled. He was trying not to cry. 'I was so scared.'

'The food's going cold,' she said.

He was still unsure. 'So what are we celebrating?'

'Eat first. Then I'll tell you.'

He gingerly put a forkful of chicken into his mouth and chewed. She could see the tension slowly leaving his body. He swallowed, took another deep breath and fanned his face with a comedy flap of his hands. 'I got a bit worked up back there.'

'There's no need to apologise.' She refilled his glass.

They ate in silence for a while. He finished the chicken and the rice and the side plate of chips. 'That was fantastic. Thank you.'

'Treacle pudding to come.'

'No expense spared.'

She put her glass down. 'But first…'

'Go on.' His face tensed again.

'Bunny Wallis…' She paused for effect. 'Will you marry me?'

He stared at her.

'Do I need to repeat the question?'

'Yes,' said Bunny. 'You do need to repeat the question.'

'Will you marry me?' She waited. 'If I have to say it a third time then I'm going to withdraw the offer.'

'Why?' asked Bunny. 'Why would you want to marry me?'

'Because I love you.'

'This is the most extraordinary day of my life.'

'Does that mean 'yes'?'

He took a deep breath. 'Of course it does. I can't imagine anything better.'

'Good.' She leant over and kissed him on the lips then sat down and poured him a third glass. 'To us.'

'To us.' He clinked his glass against hers and drank. She could see tears forming in the corners of his eyes. He said, 'I have never been this happy. Never.'

She stood up. 'I think that calls for treacle pudding.'

When she came back into the room his eyes were closed. She set the bowls down and stroked his forearm. 'Bunny?'

'I just...' He shook his head like a dog coming out of a pond. 'I'm so sorry. You ask me to marry you and I fall asleep.'

'You're tired, that's all.' She handed him the treacle pudding.

He was squeezing his eyes shut and opening them again, trying to focus. He filled his spoon with pudding and custard and lifted it halfway to his mouth but had to put it down again. 'Can you…?' He gave her the bowl. Taking his hand away he knocked the spoon onto the bedcovers. 'Shit. Sorry.'

'It's no problem.'

He leaned back and closed his eyes once more. She licked the spoon and scraped the dropped food back into the bowl. She dipped the corner of a serviette into her glass of water and rubbed gently at the stain. She squeezed his hand. 'How are you doing in there?' He squeezed back then slowly loosened his grip. She took the bowls into the kitchen, dumped the remaining treacle pudding into the bin and set the bowls in the sink. She went back into the living room and watched Bunny for a while.

'Let's make you more comfortable.' She put her hand behind his neck, pulled him forward and slipped the top pillow out from behind his head. He roused himself a little then became still. She waited for thirty seconds then pulled him forward once more to remove the next pillow. The third and last was harder to remove. Gently, she eased it free by pulling it from side to side, taking care not to wake him, until it slipped out.

He was now lying flat on his back. His breathing stopped for a few seconds then restarted. His arms circled, reaching for some invisible thing just above the bed, then they were still again. A couple of minutes later he went through the same cycle without waking. 'Bunny?' she said quietly, but there was no response.

Quarter past eight. She waited till half past. The periods when he was not breathing grew longer but some automatic response kicked in every time. Had she miscalculated? Eight forty. She put her hand on his arm. 'Come on, Bunny. Help me out here.'

Eight forty-five. He was no longer lifting his arms off the bed; just the ghost of a movement. He looked shattered, as if he were reaching the end of a long fight against a much stronger opponent.

'It's OK, Bunny. You can let go.'

She could no longer see his chest rising and falling. She could no longer hear him breathing, only a tiny, broken hiss that stopped and started and stopped and started and finally, just before nine o'clock, stopped altogether.

She waited another five minutes to be sure, then she leant over and kissed him. It was nothing, really, when you thought about it, like turning off a light. You were here, then you were gone.

She took the little brown tub from her pocket, unscrewed the lid and gently dropped both of them onto the carpet on the far side of the bed. She poured the remains of his wine onto the side table and laid the glass on its side. She carried her own glass into the kitchen where she washed the crockery, cutlery and glassware and left it to dry.

She double-bagged the packaging and the uneaten food and dropped everything in the bin outside the front door. She washed and dried her hands and went into the garden for a cigarette.

She would discover him when she came down in the morning. She would notice the glass but she would fail to see the Diazepam. She would check his pulse and his breathing but she would know from the look of him that he had been dead for some time. She would call an ambulance and wait outside for it to arrive. She would call Bunny's mother. She would call Bunny's sister. She would say, 'He seemed so happy.' She would wrap the owl and the apostle spoons and the wall plate in newspaper and put them at the bottom of her suitcase. But she wouldn't leave town till after the funeral. The idea of him being rolled through those curtains without a friend in the room was almost unbearable.

Broderie Anglaise

Frances Leviston

I WAS NOT MAID of honour, not even a bridesmaid, but I was dutifully invited, and for this I needed something suitable to wear, something that would signal my grasp of the occasion as well as my transcendence of it; but no matter where I looked – and I spent hours looking – the dress did not exist. No shop possessed it. There is no point explaining now exactly what I had in mind. The details in themselves do not matter, except to say this dress should accommodate my chest without looking matronly or profane; that it should upstage the bridal gown without appearing to do so; and that I was not exactly conscious of these obstinate stipulations, but clicked through the rails of department stores in an agitated dream, like someone brainwashed to accomplish a murder without their consent.

My solution, in the end, was to make the dress myself. At university, I had done quite a lot of sewing. Gemma, one of my housemates, owned a little sewing machine she taught me how to use, though she hardly used it herself. I would run up silly costumes for my friends for Halloween, and basic items for me. 'Run up' was a phrase of my mother's, one I tried not to use, not out loud at least, though it was stuck firmly to the walls of my mind, like the Blu Tack I had used in my rented room, the greasy little coins from which cost me my deposit. But since I had come back to my parents' house the previous summer, the sewing kit had stayed packed away, along with all the items it helped me manufacture. I didn't want to talk about it; I didn't want my mother to know.

Little by little, then, I decided I would make the dress in secret, and pretend it was vintage: my mother's side of the family did not approve of second-hand shopping, and Candice was her niece, her younger sister Amanda's child. My hopeless lunch-break expeditions down the high street became quiet pilgrimages to haberdashery departments, in which I kept my head down, moving quietly among the middle-aged and elderly ladies rattling their knuckles through trays of beads, drawing no more attention than I could help, and asking no questions in case I brought an avalanche of answers down on my head.

Many fabrics presented themselves, and I chose as carefully as I could, avoiding jersey, silk and satin because they would be too difficult to work, and linen because it would crease. Some bolts of beautiful patterned cotton I put back because I would not be able to make their bold edges join in any logical progression at the seams, or so I told myself, though I think I also quailed at the prospect of them drawing Candice's wedding guests' eyes towards me in the way they had drawn my own. After a few trips, I had amassed in my bedroom three metres of broderie anglaise, two kinds of thread, a roll of greaseproof paper, a pattern, and a roll of calico for practising with, which, along with the sewing kit I dug out from the bottom of the wardrobe, should have been everything I was going to need. Everything, that is, but the sewing machine.

Gemma lived two hundred miles away, and we had not spoken since our final exams. I knew nobody else except my mother who owned a machine. Buying one of my own would have been prohibitively expensive: I was temping as a secretary at the time, work which somehow contrived to pay slightly less than minimum wage, and what I didn't surrender in room and board to my parents was digging me out of an overdraft the bank kept threatening to dissolve. Even if I could have got my hands on my own machine, they were terribly noisy, which left me the same problems I would face if I chose to use my mother's: namely, finding a time when I could sew without detection.

As I mulled this problem over, I was not idle: I did as much as I could behind closed doors, in my bedroom, which had barely changed in my three years away, except that a chest emptied of clothes had been removed to my brother's room. This gave me more space to spread my materials out. I measured myself several times with a floppy fabric tape measure, bust and waist, hips and shoulders. I cut greaseproof panels and tacked them together, then calico panels, and slipped the rig gingerly over my head, warming to the tiny adjustable demands of my ambition, whilst downstairs my mother cooked dinners from which I excused myself, or watched one of the police dramas she liked so much, and my brother lay lost in the violent immersive dreams of his video-games.

Candice and her mother, my Auntie Manda, were often round at our house, ostensibly for the purposes of wedding planning, but also to bask in my mother's envy (the whole marriage business ran on envy, it seemed to me, like a car running on fumes). If I left my door ajar, which I could safely do when there was company downstairs, I could clearly hear them talking above the hiss and snip of the scissors.

'I went to that bakery you told me about,' Candice might say, addressing my mother, who for someone professing not to like cake had been surprisingly full of suggestions, 'and we tried a few samples, didn't we, but the quality just wasn't that good.'

'Much too sweet,' Auntie Manda would agree, sounding faintly offended. 'Really sickly.'

'Well, I thought that might be the case,' my mother would say. 'I've seen some very good things from there, and some not so good, and I thought it might be worth trying, at least, but I thought probably, probably it wouldn't be exactly what you were after.'

'No, it wasn't what we were after,' Auntie Manda would affirm. 'But then we tried the place that Susan suggested, and you liked that one a lot, didn't you, love?'

'I *really* liked that one,' Candice said, drawing out the vowels.

'They did the most beautiful icing,' Auntie Manda said. 'Really beautiful. And the sponge was very moist.'

'Well, that's what you want, isn't it,' my mother said. 'There's nothing worse than dry cake that's too sweet. I'm not a fan of cake, but I know you don't want that.'

'How can you not like cake?' Candice exclaimed. 'These cakes were beautiful. You've got to have a piece at the wedding.'

So it went, the horse-trading of preference and information, with my mother rubbed sore between her sister and niece until it was time for them to hurry away for another appointment, another opportunity to exhibit their harassment and good fortune, at which point my mother would be able to wash her hands of the whole thing; and although she was reluctant to do this – she wanted, more than anything, I think, to be right at the centre of the wedding – she could at least draw strength from her freedom.

'Lovely to see you,' she would say, trailing them down the hall. 'We'll talk tomorrow. Gosh, you've got so much to do. I don't envy you all that, I really don't. It's a bit like someone else's baby for me. I get to play with her for a while, but then I can give her back!'

They laughed at this – they always laughed – knowing full well that my mother would never have given the baby back if she did not have to. Then their laughter mutated into cries of farewell before the closing door cut them off; and although my mother stood on the near side of this door, her own cries always cut off at exactly the same moment. Then, before she could turn and climb the stairs, I would shut my own door as well. If this seems cruel, I can only say that my mother's weakness in the presence of her sister and her niece filled me not with pity but annoyance – I could not understand why she endured it. What did she think was going to change?

When I could not procrastinate any longer, I gave up the idea of using a machine and began to hand-sew the dress. It was a slow business, very slow indeed. I was not schooled in the art of invisible stitching, only the rough tacks I used to hold the pattern pieces together, and I practised on the calico and then on cuttings from the broderie anglaise before I trusted myself to touch the dress itself. I did this in the hour before and after work, because of the light, and because my mother was generally occupied at those moments, asleep or making dinner. The more time I spent with the fabric, the more enamoured I became of my choice. It was a pale, almost an unnoticeable blue, light as winter sky, the sort of colour that did not declare itself but which would make any off-whites or creams placed beside it look like old dentures in a water-glass. The delicate cut-work, scatterings of eyelets lined with satiny buttonhole-stitch, receded at distance to no more than a texture, which meant I would not have to worry about the pattern matching up; but closer in it reminded me of bubbles, or birds' prints in snow, and underneath my fingertips it leapt and swirled like a romantic dialect of Braille.

Although I could often avoid Candice when she came round, there was no avoiding the hen party, which took place a week before the wedding. Candice's maid of honour, an old school friend called Katie, had arranged for us to stay the night at a good hotel in town – our own town, that is, not anywhere else. This seemed to me absurd, and I made the mistake of saying so in the early planning stages, threatening to take a cab home at the end of the night, which set Katie and myself at odds with one another for the rest of the affair. Katie, in fact, was the darling of the party, not Candice; she decked Candice out in a polyester veil and tiara, with a plastic penis on a chain around her neck, then steered her through the streets of the city, one bar to the next, using the dazzle of Candice's appearance to reflect attention on to herself. I was reminded of a queen and her adviser, the one wielding more effectual power than the other, who sits like a fairy on the top of a tinselled tree. Men bantered with Candice as a formality, while Katie sat quietly behind her, waiting to receive her own, more valuable tributes.

At two in the morning, in the hotel bar, I finally spoke to Candice.

'Are you scared?' I asked.

'Of what? Getting married?' Her make-up had slid, her tiara was crooked, and since the shots in Walkabout she had been unable to focus. 'Fuck yeah. But I love him. I love him, you know? And being in love – it's scary.'

Drink had made her honest; for a moment I luxuriated in the false warmth of her confidence, and felt a small flicker of pity, of cousinly love.

'What are you asking her that for?' Katie interrupted.

'It's OK,' Candice said, with a slow wave of her hand.

'No, it's not. She's trying to upset you. What else have you said?'

'Nothing. It was just a question.'

'Well, don't ask her any more questions. You don't want to think about that tonight, do you, babe?'

'She's always asking questions,' Candice said. Her eyes seemed suddenly to close on me, like the fingers of a palsied hand coming together in a grip. 'She's clever.'

'Not that clever,' Katie said, 'if she's asking you questions like that.' She took hold of Candice by the wrist and led her away.

When I returned home the following morning, after barely sleeping in the plush hotel, I drew my half-finished dress from the wardrobe drawer where I kept it, wrapped tight in a Debenhams carrier bag, and held it up to the clear summer light. The hem around the bottom rippled. There were tiny puckers in the seams, nothing to which you could point close up, but which gave a slightly lopsided air to the dress's proportions. I immediately tore out all the stitches I had done by hand. There was no way around it: I would have to use my mother's machine.

The machine was a Singer from the 1970s, and it lived in its carrying-case in the cupboard under the stairs. My mother still used it fairly regularly, to make baby clothes for anyone she knew was having a baby, and for occasional repairs, but in years gone by she had made all kinds of things with it, things I still shuddered to imagine myself wearing, but which had at the time seemed like miracles to me: cord dungarees, a little cotton skirt with elastic in the waist. As a child, I had watched in impatient fascination as she heaved the machine on to the kitchen table and proceeded to fiddle with the many knobs and dials that encrusted its beige plastic casing, to open the secret hatch that caught the pins, and to wind and unwind the bobbin at top speed with the treadle. This preparatory stage always took more time than the sewing itself, provided the material didn't bunch up as she passed it beneath the needle, or where the needle was supposed to be, since it moved up and down so fast that it seemed to vanish.

Because my mother had retired early, for reasons she never explained to us, finding time alone with the machine was a challenge. I feigned illness and stayed in bed, abandoning the temporary contract I was under, which meant submitting to endless cups of tea and bowls of soup as I lay on my bed. The sharp words of my handler at the agency reverberated in my head: despite my education, I had proven myself to be just another one of those unreliable girls. A blackbird sang loudly and variously outside my window. And still my mother did not leave the house.

Many implausible courses of action crossed my mind. I could create some kind of decoy that would draw her away, maybe sending her out for a particular item that could only be located a long drive from home, or arranging for a friend to require her help; I could actually call Gemma (and say what?); I could try a school or college, which would surely have rooms full of such machines going unused over the summer; I could move out of my parents' house and dedicate a table to sewing in my new abode. I had a lot of time to consider these plans, but they always dwindled away to nothing or collapsed under the weight of their own demands. I began to feel as ill as I pretended to be. I welcomed the tea, the soup. My determination not to involve my mother in the process of making the dress, which had been a source of pride in the project's early stages, became the strong light under which my cowardice was fully revealed. While my mother went about her ordinary business downstairs, whatever that might have been, I lay mutinous and unhappy in the chamber of my adolescence, under the same ceiling I had stared at for years, half-making plans that withered and died in the face of her habitual existence.

'How are you feeling this morning?' she would ask, advancing forward into the sickbed dusk of my room and hovering there, in a light-coloured blouse, like the moon. If I rebuffed her concern, she would turn away, with a pained look on her face, and say, very reasonably, 'Alright, I'll leave you to it. Just call if you need anything.' But if I did not demonstrate quite so clearly my desire to be left alone, she would sink down on the edge of my bed, which tipped the whole mattress towards her, and update me on the wedding. The visits from Candice and Auntie Manda had stopped, now the date was imminent, but she still had plenty to say. 'The flower-shop overcharged for the bride's bouquet, did I tell you? They thought she wanted roses, so they charged her for roses, but she didn't, she wanted carnations. Manda says Candice lost six pounds in the last two weeks and they had to get her corset taken in again at the last minute.

Uncle David cried at the rehearsal...'

Still half asleep, reclining in the safety of my illness, I let the talk wash over me, and found it mattered less, bothered me less, than it had before, when I had been so determined to counteract it by bringing to the wedding something of which my mother would not know in advance. The headache I had invented grew stronger. With only a couple of days to go, I found myself in tears: she was looking after me, in her own, familiar way, and wasn't that all she wanted to do? What, exactly, was wrong with me – why did I hate her for being interested in other people's lives? Wasn't I angry that she wasn't more interested in mine? It was true that when she sat on my bed she rarely asked a question, unless it was about the severity of my pain, or whether I thought I was going to be well enough to attend the service; but that was a kind of anxious sympathy in itself, not to bother me with talking if I'd rather not speak... There was a strange, sticky quality to these feelings, like a sweet I had found unwrapped in a hidden pocket of my bag, half-melted by its contact with the air and speckled with fluff and dirt. Nevertheless, I put the sweet in my mouth.

'I've been making a dress,' I told her, surprising myself with my confession. 'It's not finished. I don't know if I'll finish it now – I needed to use your sewing machine, and then I got ill.'

She looked at me, astonished. 'You've been making a dress?'

'Yes. To wear to the wedding.'

'Where is it? Can I see it?' She looked around the room, as if it might have been hanging in plain sight all along.

'It's in the wardrobe,' I said, feeling shabby.

'Oh.' She pursed her lips. 'Well, if you feel like showing it to me, I'd like to see it.'

'I would like to show it to you. That's why I brought it up.'

'Shall I get it? Is it hidden? I don't like to rummage through your things.'

'It's in the drawer. In a Debenhams bag.'

Misgivings had already surged through me. As I watched her bend down with some difficulty to open the drawer and retrieve the bag, the headache from which I had genuinely suffered seemed to fade, and a different kind of ache took its place, one much harder to position. She came back to the bed and drew the dress from the bag.

'It's lovely material,' she said. 'Can I draw the curtains?'

Without waiting for an answer, she tore the curtains back from the window, and that same summery light flooded in. I saw the dress clearly in her hands, the fabric she had complimented now diminished in my estimation, limp and blue and childish, like the skirt she had made for me so many years before. But it was too late to stop; soon we were talking through the problems I had experienced with hand-sewing, and the modifications I had made to the pattern I bought, which were designed to nip the dress in firmly at the waist, giving more support.

She insisted we check all my measurements before she would get the sewing machine out. I found myself standing in the middle of my room, my mother's cool hands looping the fabric tape measure around my ribs beneath my pyjamas.

'You haven't allowed that much for the seams,' she said. 'I'd let out another half inch or so. You don't want to do all that sewing then find you can't zip it up.'

'The seams are fine,' I said, not wanting to tell her that I'd done this kind of thing before, that I knew my measurements precisely, though surely my possession of a tape measure and a sewing kit must have stirred her suspicions. If they did, she didn't mention it.

'They seem very slim,' she insisted.

'They're fine.'

'In that case,' she said, pursing her lips again, 'it should be quite simple. Just a straight stitch here and here' – she pointed – 'and zig zag for the rest. Shall I set up the machine? Do you want me to do it? It's just that machine's a bit tricky if you haven't used it before. It can chew things up. I wouldn't want you chewing your lovely material.'

'Is it really that bad?'

'Well, yes,' she said, turning away, 'it's chewed a few things of mine before. But it's your dress – it's really up to you.'

I showered, then, trying to wash the last of the illness away. When I came downstairs the sewing machine was out on the kitchen table, all plugged in and ready to go. I saw my own thread on the bobbin.

'I said I'd do it.'

'I heard the water running,' she said. 'I thought I could save you some time.'

I sat down in front of the shining machine, which was three times the size of Gemma's, and looked so heavy it must have immobilised the table under its weight. There was sweat on my mother's hairline from the effort of setting it up. I couldn't see a manual.

'I'll just show you,' she said, pointing over my shoulder. 'See, this is your straight switch and your zig zag switch. This is your speed – I keep it on six. And this is your reverse, for finishing off. The treadle's quite sensitive so you need a gentle foot.'

Once I ignored all the extra buttons and switches, it wasn't that different from Gemma's. Once I'd had a quick practice on some calico ('Gentle foot!'), I was ready to try the dress; but the bumpy broderie was a trickier proposition, and almost as soon as I had begun it did exactly what my mother had predicted: some part of the cut-work got caught on the needle, and the fabric was drawn up rapidly into a scrunch.

My mother, who had been pretending to read the paper across the kitchen, instantly reappeared at my side. 'Yes, that's what it tends to do,' she said. 'Broderie can be quite difficult to work with. I was worried about that.' She handed me a little tool for cutting stitches. It took me ten minutes to unpick the ravelled threads. 'Shall we have another try?' she said, when she saw me smooth it out at last. 'I could help. It's no bother. I've finished what I wanted to do.'

'No thank you,' I said. 'I'll do it.'

'I'm just worried that the mistakes are going to start showing soon. I know it's forgiving, the broderie, but probably only up to a certain point. And you've chosen quite a difficult pattern. Do you want me to try?'

I didn't answer. She stood for a moment behind me – I could feel her impatience build – and then she left the kitchen without another word. I sighed heavily: my breath steamed the chrome panel of the Singer's nameplate. The long needle gleamed, poised to descend, and the broderie lay pooled beneath it where I had lined it up to try again. The kitchen was quiet now she had gone, but I didn't move. I was afraid that I was going to ruin the dress, and afraid that I no longer cared – that, no matter how the dress turned out, I had tainted it by breaking the seal on my secret. The clock ticked loudly on the wall above the sink. I heard drawers opening and closing in another room and then I heard my mother's footsteps on the stairs, coming down the hall to the kitchen.

'This is the only other broderie I've got,' she said, in a put-upon voice, as if I had asked her to fetch it. She was out of breath. A garment appeared at my elbow, folded: white broderie anglaise, turning creamy with age. Some kind of old baby's gown. 'You can practice with it, if you want. It doesn't matter. I don't want you ruining your dress.'

'What is it?' I asked. It looked delicate and sentimental.

'Oh, it's nothing. Just your Grandma's christening gown.'

'Really?' I was genuinely surprised; I hadn't even known she possessed such things. 'God, I can't practise on that.'

'Why not?' She shook it out and held it up. Dots of dust swam in the light. It was so small; smaller than any of my own baby clothes, or the baby clothes I'd seen my mother make. 'It's the same kind of material. There's enough.'

'Doesn't it mean something to you? You've kept it this long.'

'No, not really. Not that much.'

I didn't believe her. The gown meant something, even if it wasn't obvious. Her offer was a trick, and either way she'd win: if I practised on the gown, and went through with it all on my own, she could console herself with her sacrifice; and if I couldn't bring myself to ruin the gown, then she could sew my dress herself. She knew I'd done nothing since she left the room. She knew I was frightened to proceed.

'If you don't want it,' I said, trying to come sideways at the problem, 'you could give it to me.' I reached for the gown, but she lifted it away.

'I didn't say I didn't want it. I said you could use it.' Now her tone was curdling from indulgence to irritation; I heard the note of warning, and I ignored it.

'What's the difference?' I asked.

'There is a difference. There's a big difference. This was your Grandma's, and I've had it a long time.'

'Exactly, so why do you want me to spoil it?'

'I don't want you to spoil your dress!'

She was flushed and angry. I looked down at my hands, obscurely angry myself, and ashamed. We stood there in silence for a minute. The prospect of refusing everything she offered, everything, for the rest of our lives, rose in front of me like the ghost of someone I hadn't even known was dead; the vision was far more frightening than the anger I felt. I said, in a sick and cowardly voice, 'I don't have anything of Grandma's. Can I see?'

She passed it to me with only the smallest of hesitations, which seemed to cement my indebtedness to her more than to demonstrate any attachment to the gown on her part. Its broderie was impossibly soft, as if it had been worn and washed and handled a thousand times, though it had probably only been used once, eighty years ago, when the vicar splashed my grandmother's head in the font, and my mother had not even been imagined. I carried it down the hall and up to my bedroom, hearing the sewing machine fire up behind me as she settled to her task. I wondered if she had ever watched her mother sew, ever sat spellbound while the needle rose and fell; and I knew that I would never ask.

Lying back down on my sick-bed, I examined the gown in more detail. It had little puffed sleeves, pin-tucks at the waist, and one mother-of-pearl button the size of an apple pip at the nape of the neck. The skirt fell long, far too long, with a starchy stiffness to it, and a hem of lace pointed like a row of incipient fangs.

My mother came upstairs an hour later with the finished dress in her arms. It had looked very small to her, she said, so she'd let the seams out after all.

The Assassination of Margaret Thatcher: August 6th 1983

Hilary Mantel

APRIL 25th 1982, DOWNING STREET: Announcement of the recapture of South Georgia, in the Falkland Islands.

Mrs Thatcher: Ladies and gentlemen, the Secretary of State for Defence has just come over to give me some very good news...

Secretary of State: The message we have got is that British troops landed on South Georgia this afternoon, shortly after 4pm London time... The commander of the operation has sent the following message: 'Be pleased to inform Her Majesty that the White Ensign flies alongside the Union Jack in South Georgia. God save the Queen.'

Mrs Thatcher: Just rejoice at that news and congratulate our forces and the marines. Goodnight, gentlemen.

Mrs Thatcher turns towards the door of No. 10 Downing Street.

Reporter: Are we going to declare war on Argentina, Mrs Thatcher?

Mrs Thatcher (pausing on her doorstep): Rejoice.

Picture first the street where she breathed her last. It is a quiet street, sedate, shaded by old trees: a street of tall houses, their façades smooth as white icing, their brickwork the colour of honey. Some are Georgian, flat-fronted. Others are Victorian, with gleaming bays. They are too big for modern households, and most of them have been cut up into flats. But this does not destroy their elegance of proportion, nor detract from the deep lustre of panelled front doors, brass-furnished and painted in navy or forest green. It is the neighbourhood's only drawback that there are more cars than spaces to put them. The residents park nose-to-tail, flaunting their permits. Those who have driveways are often blocked into them. But they are patient householders, proud of their handsome street and willing to suffer to live there. Glancing up, you notice a fragile Georgian fanlight, or a warm scoop of terracotta tiling, or a glint of coloured glass. In spring, cherry trees toss extravagant flounces of blossom. When the wind strips the petals, they flurry in pink drifts and carpet the pavements, as if giants have held a wedding in the street. In summer, music floats from open windows: Vivaldi, Mozart, Bach.

The street itself describes a gentle curve, joining the main road as it flows out of town. The Holy Trinity church, islanded, is hung with garrison flags. Looking from a high window over the town (as I did that day of the killing) you feel the close presence of fortress and castle. Glance to your left, and the Round Tower looms into view, pressing itself against the panes. But on days of drizzle and drifting cloud the keep diminishes, like an amateur drawing half-erased. Its lines soften, its edges fade; it shrinks into the raw cold from the river, more like a shrouded mountain than a castle built for kings.

The houses on the right-hand side of Trinity Place – I mean, on the right-hand side as you face out of town – have large gardens, each now shared between three or four tenants. In the early 1980s, England had not succumbed to the smell of burning. The carbonised reek of the weekend barbecue was unknown, except in the riverside gin palaces of Maidenhead and Bray. Our gardens, though immaculately kept, saw little footfall; there were no children in the street, just young couples who had yet to breed and older couples who might, at most, open a door to let an evening party spill out on to a terrace. Through warm afternoons the lawns baked unattended, and cats curled snoozing in the crumbling topsoil of stone urns. In autumn, leaf-heaps composted themselves on sunken patios, and were shovelled up by irritated owners of basement flats. The winter rains soaked the shrubberies, with no one there to see.

But in the summer of 1983 this genteel corner, bypassed by shoppers and tourists, found itself a focus of national interest. Behind the gardens of No. 20 and No. 21 stood the grounds of a private hospital, a graceful pale building occupying a corner site. Three days before her assassination, the prime minister entered this hospital for minor eye surgery. Since then, the area had been dislocated. Strangers jostled residents. Newspapermen and TV crews blocked the street and parked without permission in driveways. You would see them trundle up and down Spinner's Walk trailing wires and lights, their gaze rolling towards the hospital gates on Clarence Road, their necks noosed by camera straps. Every few minutes they would coagulate in a mass of heaving combat jackets, as if to reassure each other that nothing was happening: but that it would happen, by and by. They waited, and while they waited they slurped orange juice from cartons and lager from cans; they ate, crumbs spilling down their fronts, soiled paper bags chucked into flowerbeds. The baker at the top of

St Leonard's Road ran out of cheese rolls by 10am and everything else by noon. Windsorians clustered on Trinity Place, shopping bags wedged on to low walls. We speculated on why we had this honour, and when she might go away.

Windsor's not what you think. It has an intelligentsia. Once you wind down from the castle to the bottom of Peascod Street, they are not all royalist lickspittles; and as you cross over the junction to St Leonard's Road, you might sniff out closet republicans. Still, it was cold comfort at the polls for the local socialists, and people murmured that it was a vote wasted; they had to show the strength of their feelings by tactical voting, and their spirit by attending outré events at the arts centre. Recently remodelled from the fire station, it was a place where self-published poets found a platform, and sour white wine was dispensed from boxes; on Saturday mornings there were classes in self-assertion, yoga and picture framing.

But when Mrs Thatcher came to visit, the dissidents took to the streets. They gathered in knots, inspecting the press corps and turning their shoulders to the hospital gates, where a row of precious parking bays were marked out and designated DOCTORS ONLY.

A woman said, 'I have a PhD, and I'm often tempted to park there.' It was early, and her loaf was still warm from the baker; she snuggled it against her, like a pet. She said, 'There are some strong opinions flying about.'

'Mine is a dagger,' I said, 'and it's flying straight to her heart.'

'Your sentiment,' she said admiringly, 'is the strongest I've heard.'

'Well, I have to go in,' I said. 'I'm expecting Mr Duggan to mend my boiler.'

'On a Saturday? Duggan? You're highly honoured. Better scoot. If you miss him he'll charge you. He's a shark, that man. But what can you do?' She fished for a pen in the bottom of her bag. 'I'll give you my number.' She wrote it on my bare arm, as neither of us had paper. 'Give me a ring. Do you ever go to the arts centre? We can get together over a glass of wine.'

I was putting my Perrier water in the fridge when the doorbell rang. I'd been thinking, we don't know it now, but we'll look back with fondness on the time Mrs Thatcher was here: new friendships formed in the street, chit-chat about plumbers whom we hold in common. On the entryphone there was the usual crackle, as if someone had set fire to the line. 'Come up, Mr Duggan,' I said. It was as well to be respectful to him.

I lived on the third floor, the stairs were steep and Duggan was ponderous. So I was surprised at how soon I heard the tap at the door. 'Hello,' I said. 'Did you manage to park your van?'

On the landing – or rather on the top step, as I was alone up there – stood a man in a cheap quilted jacket. My innocent thought was, here is

Duggan's son. 'Boiler?' I said.

'Right,' he said.

He heaved himself in, with his boiler man's bag. We were nose to nose in the box-sized hall. His jacket, more than adequate to the English summer, took up the space between us. I edged backwards. 'What's up with it?' he said.

'It groans and bangs. I know it's August, but –'

'No, you're right, you're right, you can never trust the weather. Rads hot?'

'In patches.'

'Air in your system,' he said. 'While I'm waiting I'll bleed it. Might as well. If you've got a key.'

It was then that a suspicion struck me. Waiting, he said. Waiting for what? 'Are you a photographer?'

He didn't answer. He was patting himself down, searching his pockets, frowning.

'I was expecting a plumber. You shouldn't just walk in.'

'You opened the door.'

'Not to you. Anyway, I don't know why you bothered. You can't see the front gates from this side. You need to go out of here,' I said pointedly, 'and turn left.'

'They say she's coming out the back way. It's a great place to get a shot.'

My bedroom had a perfect view of the hospital garden; anyone, by walking around the side of the house, could guess this.

'Who do you work for?' I said.

'You don't need to know.'

'Perhaps not, but it would be polite to tell me.'

As I backed into the kitchen, he followed. The room was full of sunlight, and now I saw him clearly: a stocky man, thirties, unkempt, with a round friendly face and unruly hair. He dumped his bag on the table, and pulled off his jacket. His size diminished by half. 'Let's say I'm freelance.'

'Even so,' I said, 'I should get a fee for the use of my premises. It's only fair.'

'You couldn't put a price on this,' he said.

By his accent, he was from Liverpool. Far from Duggan, or Duggan's son. But then he hadn't spoken till he was in at the front door, so how could I have known? He could have been a plumber, I said to myself. I hadn't been a total fool; for the moment, self-respect was all that concerned me. Ask for identification, people advise, before letting a stranger in. But imagine the ruckus that Duggan would have caused, if you'd held his boy up on the stairs, impeding him from getting to the next boiler on his list, and shortening his plunder opportunities.

The kitchen window looked down over Trinity Place, now seething with people. If I craned my neck I could see a new police presence to my left, trotting up from the private gardens of Clarence Crescent. 'Have one of these?' The visitor had found his cigarettes.

'No. And I'd rather you didn't.'

'Fair enough.' He crushed the pack into his pocket, and pulled out a balled-up handkerchief. He stood back from the tall window, mopping his face; face and handkerchief were both crumpled and grey. Clearly it wasn't something he was used to, tricking himself into private houses. I was more annoyed with myself than with him. He had a living to make, and perhaps you couldn't blame him for pushing in, when some fool of a woman held the door open. I said, 'How long do you propose to stay?'

'She's expected in an hour.'

'Right.' That accounted for it, the increased hum and buzz from the street. 'How do you know?'

'We've a girl on the inside. A nurse.'

I handed him two sheets of kitchen roll. 'Ta.' He blotted his forehead. 'She's going to come out and the doctors and nurses are lining up, so she can appreciate them. She's going to walk along the line with her thank-you and bye-bye, then toddle round the side, duck into a limo and she's away. Well, that's the idea. I don't have an exact time. So I thought if I was here early I could set up, have a look at the angles.'

'How much will you get for a good shot?'

'Life without parole,' he said.

I laughed. 'It's not a crime.'

'That's my feeling.'

'It's a fair distance,' I said. 'I mean, I know you have special lenses, and you're the only one up here, but don't you want a close-up?'

'Nah,' he said. 'As long as I get a clear view, the distance is a doddle.'

He crumpled up the kitchen roll and looked around for the bin. I took the paper from him, he grunted, then applied himself to unstrapping his bag, a canvas holdall that I supposed would be as suitable for a photographer as for any tradesman. But one by one he took out metal parts which, even in my ignorance, I knew were not part of a photographer's kit. He began to assemble them; his fingertips were delicate. As he worked he sang, almost under his breath, a little song from the football terraces:

'You are a scouser, a dirty scouser,
You're only happy on giro day.
Your dad's out stealing, your mam's
        drug-dealing,
Please don't take our hub-caps away.'

'Three million unemployed,' he said. 'Most of them live round our way. It wouldn't be a problem here, would it?'

'Oh no. Plenty of gift shops to employ everybody. Have you been up to the High Street?'

I thought of the tourist scrums pushing each other off the pavements, jostling for souvenir humbugs and wind-up Beefeaters. It could have been another country. No voices carried from the street below. Our man was humming, absorbed. I wondered if his song had a second verse. As he lifted each component from his bag he wiped it with a cloth that was cleaner than his handkerchief, handling it with gentle reverence, like an altar boy polishing the vessels for mass.

When the mechanism was assembled he held it out for my inspection. 'Folding stock,' he said. 'That's the beauty of her. Fits in a cornflakes packet. They call her the widowmaker. Though not in this case. Poor bloody Denis, eh? He'll have to boil his own eggs from now on.'

It feels, in retrospect, as if hours stretched ahead, as we sat in the bedroom together, he on a folding chair near the sash window, his mug of tea cradled in his hands, the widowmaker at his feet; myself on the edge of the bed, over which I had hastily dragged the duvet to tidy it. He had brought his jacket from the kitchen; perhaps the pockets were crammed with assassin's requisites. When he flung it on the bed, it slid straight off again. I tried to grab it and my palm slid across the nylon; like a reptile, it seemed to have its own life. I flumped it on the bed beside me and took a grip on it by the collar. He looked on with mild approval.

He kept glancing at his watch, though he said he had no certain time. Once he rubbed its face with his palm, as if it might be fogged and concealing a different time underneath. He would check, from the corner of his eye, that I was still where I should be, my hands in view: as, he explained, he preferred them to be. Then he would fix his gaze on the lawns, the back fences. As if to be closer to his target, he rocked his chair forwards on its front legs.

I said, 'It's the fake femininity I can't stand, and the counterfeit voice. The way she boasts about her dad the grocer and what he taught her, but you know she would change it all if she could, and be born to rich people. It's the way she loves the rich, the way she worships them. It's her philistinism, her ignorance, and the way she revels in her ignorance. It's her lack of pity. Why does she need an eye operation? Is it because she can't cry?'

When the telephone rang, it made us both jump. I broke off what I was saying. 'Answer that,' he said. 'It will be for me.'

It was hard for me to imagine the busy network of activity that lay behind the day's plans. 'Wait,' I'd said to him, as I asked him, 'Tea or coffee?' as I switched the kettle on. 'You know I was expecting the boiler man? I'm sure he'll be here soon.'

'Duggan?' he said. 'Nah.'

'You know Duggan?'

'I know he won't be here.'

'What have you done to him?'

'Oh, for God's sake.' He snorted. 'Why would we do anything? No need. He got the nod. We have pals all over the place.'

Pals. A pleasing word. Almost archaic. Dear God, I thought, Duggan an IRA man. Not that my visitor had named his affiliation, but I had spoken it loudly in my mind. The word, the initials, didn't cause me the shock or upset it would cause, perhaps, to you. I told him this, as I reached in the fridge for milk and waited for the kettle to boil: saying, I would deter you if I could, but it would only be out of fear for myself and what's going to happen to me after you've done it: which by the way is what? I am no friend of this woman, though I don't (I felt compelled to add) believe violence solves anything. But I would not betray you, because...

'Yeah,' he said. 'Everybody's got an Irish granny. It's no guarantee of anything at all. I'm here for your sightlines. I don't care about your affinities. Keep away from the front window and don't touch the phone, or I'll knock you dead. I don't care about the songs your bloody great-uncles used to sing on a Saturday night.'

I nodded. It was only what I'd thought myself. It was sentiment and no substance.

> 'The minstrel boy to the war is gone,
> In the ranks of death you'll find him.
> His father's sword he has girded on,
> And his wild harp slung behind him.'

My great-uncles (and he was right about them) wouldn't have known a wild harp if it had sprung up and bitten their bottoms. Patriotism was only an excuse to get what they called pie-eyed, while their wives had tea and gingernuts then recited the rosary in the back kitchen. The whole thing was an excuse: why we are oppressed. Why we are sat here being oppressed, while people from other tribes are hauling themselves up by their own ungodly efforts and buying three-piece suites. While we are rooted here going la-la-la auld Ireland (because at this distance in time the words escape us) our neighbours are patching their quarrels, losing their origins and moving on, to modern, non-sectarian forms of stigma, expressed in modern songs: you are a scouser, a dirty scouser. I'm not, personally. But the north is all the same to southerners. And in Berkshire and the Home Counties, all causes are the same, all ideas for which a person might care to die: they are nuisances, a breach of the peace, and likely to hold up the traffic or delay the trains.

'You seem to know about me,' I said. I sounded resentful.

'As much as anybody would need to know. That's to say, not that you're anything special. You can be a help if you want, and if you don't want, we can do accordingly.'

He spoke as if he had companions. He was only one man. But a bulky one, even without the jacket. Suppose I had been a true-blue Tory, or one of those devout souls who won't so much as crush an insect: I still wouldn't have tried anything tricky. As it was, he counted on me to be docile, or perhaps, despite his sneering, he trusted me to some small extent. Anyway, he let me follow him into the bedroom with my mug of tea. He carried his own tea in his left hand and his gun in his right.

He left the roll of sticky tape and the handcuffs on the kitchen table, where he'd put them when they came out of his bag.

And now he let me pick up the phone extension from the bedside table, and hand it to him. I heard a woman's voice, young, timid and far away. You would not have thought she was in the hospital round the corner. 'Brendan?' she said. I did not imagine that was his real name.

He put down the receiver so hard it clattered. 'There's some friggin' hold-up. It'll be twenty minutes, she reckons. Or thirty, it could even be thirty.' He let his breath out, as if he'd been holding it since he stomped upstairs. 'Bugger this. Where's the lav?'

You can surprise a person with 'affinity', I thought, and then say, 'Where's the lav?' Not a Windsor expression. It wasn't really a question, either. The flat was so small that its layout was obvious. He took his weapon with him. I listened to him urinate. Run a tap. I heard splashing. I heard him come out, zipping his trousers. His face was red where he'd been towelling it. He sat down hard on the folding chair. There was a bleat from the fragile canework. He said, 'You've got a number written on your arm.'

'Yes.'

'What's it a number of?'

'A woman.' I dabbed my forefinger with my tongue and slicked it across the ink.

'You won't get it off that way. You need to get some soap and give it a good scrub.'

'How kind of you to take an interest.'

'Have you wrote it down? Her number?'

'No.'

'Don't you want it?'

Only if I have a future, I thought. I wondered when it would be appropriate to ask.

'Make us another brew. And put sugar in it this time.'

'Oh,' I said. I was flustered by a failing in hospitality. 'I didn't know you took sugar. I might not have white.'

'The bourgeoisie, eh?'

I was angry. 'You're not too proud to shoot out of my bourgeois sash window, are you?'

He lurched forward, hand groping for the gun. It wasn't to shoot me, though my heart leapt. He glared down into the gardens, tensing as if he were going to butt his head through the glass. He made a small, dissatisfied grunt, and sat down again. 'A bloody cat on the fence.'

'I have demerara,' I said. 'I expect it tastes the same, when it's stirred in.'

'You wouldn't think of shouting out of the kitchen window, would you?' he said. 'Or trying to bolt down the stairs?'

'What, after all I've said?'

'You think you're on my side?' He was sweating again. 'You don't know my side. Believe me, you have no idea.'

It crossed my mind then he might not be a Provisional, but from one of the mad splinter groups you heard of. I was hardly in a position to quibble; the end result would be the same. But I said, 'Bourgeoisie, what sort of polytechnic expression is that?'

I was insulting him, and I meant to. For those of tender years, I should explain that polytechnics were institutes of higher education, for the young who missed university entrance: for those who were bright enough to say 'affinity', but still wore cheap nylon coats.

He frowned. 'Brew the tea.'

'I don't think you should sneer at my great-uncles for being cod-Irish, if you talk in slogans you found in skips.'

'It was a sort of a joke,' he said.

'Oh. Well. Was it?' I was taken aback. 'It looks as if I've no more sense of humour than she has.'

I indicated, with my head, the lawns outside the window, where the prime minister was shortly to die.

'I don't fault her for not laughing,' he said. 'I won't fault her for that.'

'You should. It's why she can't see how ridiculous she is.'

'I wouldn't call her ridiculous,' he said, mulish. 'Cruel, wicked, but not ridiculous. What's there to laugh at?'

'All things human laugh,' I said.

After some thought, he replied, 'Jesus wept.'

He smirked. I saw he had relaxed, knowing that because of the friggin' delay he wouldn't have to murder yet. 'Mind you,' I said, 'she'd probably laugh if she were here. She'd laugh because she despises us. Look at your anorak. She despises your anorak. Look at my hair. She despises my hair.'

He glanced up. He'd not looked at me before, not to see me; I was just the tea-maker. 'The way it just hangs there,' I explained. 'Instead of being in corrugations. I ought to have it washed and set. It ought to go in graduated rollers, she knows where she is with that sort of hair. And I don't like the way she walks. 'Toddles', you said. 'She'll toddle round.' You had it right, there.'

'What do you think this is about?' he said.

'Ireland.'

He nodded. 'And I want you to understand that. I'm not shooting her because she doesn't like the opera. Or because you don't care for – what in sod's name do you call it? – her accessories. It's not about her handbag. It's not about her hairdo. It's about Ireland. Only Ireland, right?'

'Oh, I don't know,' I said. 'You're a bit of a fake yourself, I think. You're no nearer the old country than I am. Your great-uncles didn't know the words either. So you might want supporting reasons. Adjuncts.'

'I was brought up in a tradition,' he said. 'And look, it brings us here.' He looked around, as if he didn't believe it: the crucial act of a dedicated life, ten minutes from now, with your back to a chipboard wardrobe glossed with white veneer; a pleated paper blind, an unmade bed, a strange woman, and your last tea with no sugar in it. 'I think of those boys on hunger strike,' he said, 'the first of them dead almost two years to the day that she was first elected: did you know that? It took sixty-six days for Bobby to die. And nine other boys not far behind him. After you've starved yourself for about forty-five days they say it gets better. You stop dry-heaving and you can take water again. But that's your last chance, because after fifty days you can hardly see or hear. Your body digests itself. It eats itself in despair. You wonder she can't laugh? I see nothing to laugh at.'

'What can I say?' I asked him. 'I agree with everything you've said. You go and make the tea and I'll sit here and mind the gun.'

For a moment, he seemed to consider it.

'You'd miss. You're not trained at all.'

'How are you trained?'

'Targets.'

'It's not like a live person. You might shoot the nurses. The doctors.'

'I might, at that.'

I heard his long, smoker's cough. 'Oh, right, the tea,' I said. 'But you know another thing? They may have been blind at the end, but their eyes were open when they went into it. You can't force pity from a government like hers. Why would she negotiate? Why would you expect it? What's a dozen Irishmen to them? What's a hundred? All those people, they're capital punishers. They pretend to be modern, but leave them to themselves and they'd gouge eyes out in the public squares.'

'It might not be a bad thing,' he said. 'Hanging. In some circumstances.'

I stared at him. 'For an Irish martyr? Okay. Quicker than starving yourself.'

'It is that. I can't fault you there.'

'You know what men say, in the pub? They say, name an Irish martyr. They say, go on, go on, you can't, can you?'

'I could give you a string of names,' he said. 'They were in the paper. Two years, is that too long to remember?'

'No. But keep up, will you? The people who say this, they're Englishmen.'

'You're right. They're Englishmen,' he said sadly. 'They can't remember bugger-all.'

★   ★   ★

Ten minutes, I thought. Ten minutes give or take. In defiance of him, I sidled up to the kitchen window. The street had fallen into its weekend torpor; the crowds were around the corner. They must be expecting her soon. There was a telephone on the kitchen worktop, right by my hand, but if I picked it up he would hear the bedroom extension give its little yip, and he would come out and kill me, not with a bullet but in some less obtrusive way that would not alert the neighbours and spoil his day.

I stood by the kettle while it boiled. I wondered: has the eye surgery been a success? When she comes out, will she be able to see as normal? Will they have to lead her? Will her eyes be bandaged?

I did not like the picture in my mind. I called out to him, to know the answer. No, he shouted back, the old eyes will be sharp as a tack.

I thought, there's not a tear in her. Not for the mother in the rain at the bus stop, or the sailor burning in the sea. She sleeps four hours a night. She lives on the fumes of whisky and the iron in the blood of her prey.

★　★　★

When I took back the second mug of tea, with the demerara stirred in, he had taken off his baggy sweater, which was unravelling at the cuffs; he dresses for the tomb, I thought, layer on layer but it won't keep out the cold. Under the wool he wore a faded flannel shirt. Its twisted collar curled up; I thought, he looks like a man who does his own laundry. 'Hostages to fortune?' I said.

'No,' he said, 'I don't get very far with the lasses.' He passed a hand over his hair to flatten it, as if the adjustment might change his fortunes. 'No kids, well, none I know of.'

I gave him his tea. He took a gulp and winced. 'After…' he said.

'Yes?'

'Right after, they'll know where the shot's come from, it won't take any time for them to work that out. Once I get down the stairs and out the front door, they'll have me right there in the street. I'm going to take the gun, so as soon as they sight me they'll shoot me dead.' He paused and then said, as if I had demurred, 'It's the best way.'

'Ah,' I said. 'I thought you had a plan. I mean, other than getting killed.'

'What better plan could I have?' There was only a touch of sarcasm. 'It's a godsend, this. The hospital. Your attic. Your window. You. It's cheap. It's clean. It gets the job done, and it costs one man.'

I had said to him earlier, violence solves nothing. But it was only a piety, like a grace before meat. I wasn't attending to its meaning as I said it, and if I thought about it, I felt a hypocrite. It's only what the strong preach to the weak: you never hear it the other way round; the strong don't lay down their arms. 'What if I could buy you a moment?'

I said. 'If you were to wear your jacket to the killing, and be ready to go: to leave the widowmaker here, and pick up your empty bag, and walk out like a boiler man, the way you came in?'

'As soon as I walk out of this house I'm done.'

'But if you were to walk out of the house next door?'

'And how would that be managed?' he said.

I said, 'Come with me.'

★   ★   ★

He was nervous to leave it, his sentry post, but on this promise he must. We still have five minutes, I said, and you know it, so come, leave your gun tidily under your chair. He crowded up behind me in the hall, and I had to tell him to step back so I could open the door. 'Put it on the latch,' he advised. 'It would be a farce if we were shut out on the stairs.'

The staircases of these houses have no daylight. You can push a time-switch on the wall and flood the landings with a yellow glare. After the allotted two minutes you will be back in the dark. But the darkness is not so deep as you first think.

You stand, breathing gently, evenly, eyes adapting. Feet noiseless on the thick carpets, descend just one half-flight. Listen: the house is silent. The tenants who share this staircase are gone all day. Closed doors annul and muffle the world outside, the cackle of news bulletins from radios, the buzz of the trippers from the top of the town, even the apocalyptic roar of the aeroplanes as they dip towards Heathrow. The air, uncirculated, has a camphor smell, as if the people who first lived here were creaking open wardrobes, lifting out their mourning clothes. Neither in nor out of the house, visible but not seen, you could lurk here for an hour undisturbed, you could loiter for a day. You could sleep here; you could dream. Neither innocent nor guilty, you could skulk here for decades, while the alderman's daughter grows old: between step and step, grow old yourself, slip the noose of your name. One day Trinity Place will fall down, in a puff of plaster and powdered bone. Time will draw to a zero point, a dot: angels will pick through the ruins, kicking up the petals from the gutters, arms wrapped in tattered flags.

On the stairs, a whispered word: 'And will you kill me?' It is a question you can only ask in the dark.

'I'll leave you gagged and taped,' he says. 'In the kitchen. You can tell them I did it the minute I burst in.'

'But when will you really do it?' Voice a murmur.

'Just before. No time after.'

'You will not. I want to see. I'm not missing this.'

'Then I'll tie you up in the bedroom, okay? I'll tie you up with a view.'

'You could let me slip downstairs just before. I'll take a shopping bag. If nobody sees me go, I'll say I was out the whole time. But make sure to force my door, won't you? Like a break-in?'

'I see you know my job.'

'I'm learning.'

'I thought you wanted to see it happen.'

'I'd be able to hear it. It'll be like the roar from the Roman circus.'

'No. We'll not do that.' A touch: hand brushing arm. 'Show me this thing. Whatever it is I'm here for, wasting time.'

On the half-landing there is a door. It looks like the door to a broom cupboard. But it is heavy. Heavy to pull, hand slipping on the brass knob.

'Fire door.'

He leans past and yanks it open.

Behind it, two inches away, another door.

'Push.'

He pushes. Slow glide, dark into matching dark. The same faint, trapped, accumulating scent, the scent of the margin where the private and public worlds meet: raindrops on contract carpet, wet umbrella, damp shoe-leather, metal tang of keys, the salt of metal in palm. But this is the house next door. Look down into the dim well. It is the same, but not. You can step out of that frame and into this. A killer, you enter No. 21. A plumber, you exit No. 20. Beyond the fire door there are other households with other lives. Different histories lie close; they are curled like winter animals, breathing shallow, pulse undetected.

What we need, it is clear, is to buy time. A few moments' grace to deliver us from a situation that seems unnegotiable. There is a quirk in the building's structure. It is a slender chance but the only one. From the house next door he will emerge a few yards nearer the end of the street: nearer the right end, away from town and castle, away from the crime. We must assume that despite his bravado he does not intend to die if he can help it: that somewhere in the surrounding streets, illegally parked in a resident's bay or blocking a resident's drive, there is a vehicle waiting for him, to convey him beyond reach, and dissolve him as if he had never been.

He hesitates, looking into the dark.

'Try it. Do not put on the light. Do not speak. Step through.'

Who has not seen the door in the wall? It is the invalid child's consolation, the prisoner's last hope. It is the easy exit for the dying man, who perishes not in the death-grip of a rattling gasp, but passes on a sigh, like a falling feather. It is a special door and obeys no laws that govern wood or iron. No locksmith can defeat it, no bailiff kick it in; patrolling policemen pass it, because it is visible only to the eye of faith. Once through it, you return as angles and air, as sparks and flame. That the assassin was a flicker in its frame, you know. Beyond the fire door he melts, and this is how you've never seen him on the news. This is how you don't know his name, his face. This is how, to your certain knowledge, Mrs Thatcher went on living till she died. But note the door: note the wall: note the power of the door in the wall that you never saw was there. And note the cold wind that blows through it, when you open it a crack. History could always have been otherwise. For there is the time, the place, the black opportunity: the day, the hour, the slant of the light, the ice-cream van chiming from a distant road near the bypass.

And stepping back, into No. 21, the assassin grunts with laughter.

'Shh!' I say.

'Is that your great suggestion? They shoot me a bit further along the street? Okay, we'll give it a go. Exit along another line. A little surprise.'

Time is short now. We return to the bedroom. He has not said if I shall live or should make other plans. He motions me to the window. 'Open it now. Then get back.'

He is afraid of a sudden noise that might startle someone below. But though the window is heavy, and sometimes shudders in its frame, the sash slides smoothly upwards. He need not fret. The gardens are empty. But over in the hospital, beyond the fences and shrubs, there is movement. They are beginning to come out: not the official party, but a gaggle of nurses in their aprons and caps.

He takes up the widowmaker, lays her tenderly across his knees. He tips his chair forward, and because I see his hands are once more slippery with sweat I bring him a towel and he takes it without speaking, and wipes his palms. Once more I am reminded of something priestly: a sacrifice. A wasp dawdles over the sill. The scent of the gardens is watery, green. The tepid sunshine wobbles in, polishes his shabby brogues, moves shyly across the surface of the dressing table. I want to ask: when what is to happen, happens, will it be noisy? From where I sit? If I sit? Or stand? Stand where? At his shoulder? Perhaps I should kneel and pray.

And now we are seconds from the target. The terrace, the lawns, are twittering with hospital personnel. A receiving line has formed. Doctors, nurses, clerks. The chef joins it, in his whites and a toque. It is a kind of hat I have only seen in children's picture books. Despite myself, I giggle. I am conscious of every rise and fall of the assassin's breath. A hush falls: on the gardens, and on us.

High heels on the mossy path. Tippy-tap. Toddle on. She's making efforts, but getting nowhere very fast. The bag on the arm, slung like a shield. The tailored suit just as I have foreseen, the pussy-cat bow, a long loop of pearls, and – a new touch – big goggle glasses. Shading her, no doubt, from the trials of the afternoon. Hand extended, she is moving along the line. Now that we are here at last, there is all the time in the world. The gunman kneels, easing into position. He sees what I see, the glittering helmet of hair. He sees it shine like a gold coin in a gutter, he sees it big as the full moon. On the sill the wasp hovers, suspends itself in still air. One easy wink of the world's blind eye: 'Rejoice,' he says. 'Fucking rejoice.'

Do it Now,
Jump the Table

Jeremy Page

STANDING ON A PETROL station forecourt in a pitch black valley in Wales, Thom remembered his girlfriend's parents liked to walk around their house naked. Well, not exactly true. Sometimes they wore clothes. Susan had given him all the necessary details, such as how her mother, Lindy, would probably be wearing an elasticated tent dress with a floral print on it, that she kept hanging on a peg in the hall, in case someone she didn't know knocked on the door. Likewise her father, Alistair, had his own peg next to hers where he hung an old pair of tennis shorts.

'Modesty clothes,' Susan had called them. 'Anyway, most likely – they'll be dressed when you turn up. So nothing to worry about.'

For Thom, *most likely* was plenty to worry about.

He pushed the nozzle of the pump into the tank and listened to the soothing gush of petrol.

The car made ticking appreciative noises as the engine cooled. He smelt the cool night air, full of the scent of rock and fir trees and peaty soil, mingling with the smell of petrol, softly rising from the nozzle. He let his finger off the pump's trigger, and stared beyond the acidic light of the forecourt into the velvet darkness of the Welsh night. He saw a bank of trees, dimly illuminated, and the beginning of a hillside, rising steeply.

The nudity wasn't the problem, he thought. It was the other thing that Susan had gone on to mention:

'What *touching*?' he'd asked.

'They might touch each other in a way that's – inappropriate.'

'How?'

'I don't know. A pat on the bum maybe.' Susan had been hesitant. 'You know – like when they're passing each other on the stairs.'

'Well – what can I say – it sounds sweet. Suse – I'm sure I'll cope.'

'Dad likes to cup her breast at the kitchen sink.'

'Right.' Thom had looked at Susan, wanting to laugh, wondering how serious he should be taking this and whether (a slight possibility) she was teasing. It was going to be the first time he met the parents.

'Just – don't make anything of it. Don't react,' she'd said.

'Keep calm and don't stare!' he'd joked. She hadn't replied. 'We don't choose our parents, do we?' he'd added, expecting her to agree. But instead she frowned, and he wondered whether she'd taken offence from an insult he hadn't meant to give.

The farmhouse was old and large and not very well lit, as if this far up the valley electricity had dwindled to a trickle. He parked the car and knocked on the door, his bags in his hands, listening to a steady string of drips falling from a downpipe. Through a panel of pebbled glass he saw Susan approaching. She opened the door and threw her arms round him. 'You got here,' she whispered. 'I can't believe you got here.'

Behind her, he saw Susan's mother take a step towards him from a back room, before she halted to let her daughter complete the hug. It was a gloomy corridor, lit by a single low energy bulb, and he couldn't see her properly.

'What have you eaten?' Susan asked.

'Crisps and chocolate. Then more crisps.'

'Right – so we need to sort you out.'

Susan brought him into the hall and called out to her mother. When Lindy came forward, he saw she was wearing the thing that must be the elasticated tent dress. It *did* have a floral print on it. Her shoulders were bare and freckled and her knees and legs looked dirty. She gave him a welcoming kiss on his cheek, holding him tight with large fleshy arms, and as she let him go, gave him a slyly appraising wink.

'Yep – he'll do, Suse,' she said.

'*Mum!*' Susan replied, giving an exaggerated roll of her eyes. 'Just *ignore* my mother, will you?' She turned to Lindy. 'And you, behave.' They had terrible fallouts, Susan had told him, but it seemed his arrival was a good time to show their love. Susan gave her mother a hug and, during an embrace that seemed to have several ritual stages of rubbing each other's backs and stroking each other's hair – Thom noticed the couple of pegs behind the door, where Lindy and Alistair's modesty covers could be hung. Both pegs were empty.

They went into a large kitchen at the back of the house. It was a cluttered room with floor to ceiling shelves loaded with saucepans and cookbooks and a long Welsh dresser rammed with stacks of paper, magazines and crockery. In one corner of the room, hardly noticeable, was an apparently naked man sitting on a Lloyd Loom chair, filling in a crossword.

'My father,' Susan introduced.

'Alistair,' the man said. He stood up to shake Thom's hand, and Thom couldn't help but drop his gaze to see the man was wearing a pair of shorts.

'Six across is a *bugger*,' Alistair said, in a soft Welsh accent.

'This man,' Lindy said, 'has never completed a crossword in his life.' She stepped over to him and pinched his nose.

'Ouch, that hurt it did,' he laughed.

'Meant to.' She cleared a box of fruit from the table and served him a bowl of bright red soup. 'Beetroot. Very delicious, but...'

'...it gives you red pee,' Alistair said.

'Yes. So don't worry.'

Susan sat next to him while he ate, mildly embarrassed while her parents continued to fuss, the father bringing him a glass of beer and the mother making him try some cheese she'd bought earlier that day. He noticed the glances the parents gave each other – little half-winks and occasional giggles. They're flirting, he thought – they're actually flirting with each other. 'You'll get used to them,' Susan said, wearily. 'These two are like a couple of teenagers.' It was said, not entirely jokingly, Thom could tell that much, and Lindy seemed to take notice, raising her eyebrows at her daughter.

'Alistair,' Lindy said in a theatrical whisper, 'let's leave the young couple to it, shall we?'

Alistair screwed his face up in delight, and jogged towards the door, light on his feet. 'Nice to meet you, Thom, we'll have some time together tomorrow,' he said. He trailed his fingers across his wife's bum as he passed. 'Right-o peaches,' he said, as they left.

Susan put her head down on the table, in mock despair.

With the parental double-act gone, it was suddenly very quiet in the kitchen.

'Did your dad just call her *peaches*?' Thom asked.

'Don't,' Susan replied.

After the soup they went up to Susan's bedroom. The farmhouse seemed to be mostly unlit, with long dingy corridors and rooms filled with heavy furniture on thin carpets. In each corner Thom expected he might see the father, ready for a late night chat, or the mother wanting to give him a crushing hug again. He was relieved to get into the bedroom, where a stereo was playing and several sidelights were left on. Clearly a freer flow of electricity was allowed in there.

He took a shower in the en suite, glad to be back with his girlfriend. Glad, too, that the parents had clearly opted to wear clothes for the weekend. Naked parents was something he wouldn't have to deal with, at least.

When he came out, Susan was already in bed. He switched the light off and got in beside her.

'Susan' he whispered, 'do you think I passed the boyfriend test?'

'You did very well.'

'What's that – a pass, a distinction?'

'I think, a merit.'

'Merit's good, right?'

'But now you're being needy.' She gave him a kiss on his forehead. Their code to let him know she wanted to sleep.

He lay back on his pillow, listening to the sound of sheep out on the hillsides, and of running water somewhere near the house. It was quiet. Thrillingly quiet. Susan began to breath deeply, and he locked his fingers into hers, thinking of the journey he'd done. He'd felt special at the petrol station. A traveller, paused. The lights of the forecourt had shone dimly off the curves of the car's roof. His car had looked, briefly, like a plane does in a hangar, full of potential, designed to move between two very different worlds. The last few miles up the valley to the farmhouse at Blaen-y-cym had been narrow, and driving it had felt like following a river to its source – the road growing ever smaller until, eventually, it had been a single lane between dry stone walls. That Susan had been here, found at the river's source seemed, as he fell asleep, to have great significance. He'd found her, in all the permutations of motorways and junctions and roads and lanes, like she'd hidden as far away as possible in an intricate puzzle.

He woke early in the bright, cold bedroom, and placed the palm of his hand on the wall next to him. It felt damp and solid. Susan was warm, deeply asleep, and he noticed she was wearing a pair of man's brushed cotton pyjamas he'd never seen before. Candy stripe. Perhaps they belonged to the father, Thom thought. He went to the window and looked outside at a vividly green Welsh valley. It was steeper and smaller than he'd imagined last night, with outcrops of dark grey rock and banks of fir trees above him. The sheep were well into their day already, dotted across the hillside, bleating to each other.

He looked back at Susan. She was lying on her back, with her mouth slightly open. When she was this fast asleep, her chin was slack and her neck looked thicker. She resembled her mother.

'You awake?' he whispered. She didn't answer. This was his girlfriend, but she seemed different from the one who rushed her breakfast in their flat in South London, who travelled on a packed tube with him, until their routes separated at Oxford Circus, him going west and her going east on the Central Line, a quick peck on the cheek in the single chamber, deep underground, where the tube lines met. Different from the girlfriend he emailed from his desk, met at restaurants, chose their Friday night takeaway with. This girl in the bed was the Welsh version of the girl he knew, who wore woollen socks to sleep in, and was curiously quiet without the endless distractions and subjects that London threw at them.

Hearing the sounds of plates being washed up, and a kettle coming to the boil, he went downstairs. Lindy was at the kitchen sink, wearing the same elasticated tent dress from the night before. He noticed the print was of small sunflowers, with tiny bees buzzing round the petals.

She gave him a broad smile, but stopped short of a hug this time. 'Will you have poached eggs?' she asked.

'Please.'

'I'll poach you a couple. And coffee, of course – you boys love your coffee, don't you. Did you sleep well?'

He nodded. 'Yes. Very.'

'This valley has a magical air, Thom. Sleep comes easy here.'

While she made the eggs she told him about moving to the house, in the early-eighties, with Susan a grubby-faced babe in arms, allowed to crawl across the flagstones and out among the sheep. How Alistair had had plans to harness the water and wind power, even back then, except his mill and wind turbine had been a beautiful but endlessly collapsing project.

'Sometimes a sheep would wander into the kitchen. It would come in here and get scared because it was in a house, so it would jump up on the table. And just stand there. Alistair – I'd go – a sheep's just jumped the table!' She sighed, in a moment of quiet contemplation. 'Sometimes you've just got to jump the table, Thom.' She held his gaze. 'None of that happens now. Even the sheep have changed – why does – why does *everything* have to change?'

He wasn't sure whether he was being asked a question.

'Now – Sue's told you we're not keen on wearing clothes?'

'Oh yeah – that – I'm fine about it.'

'We can keep these things on if you'd rather? We don't want you to feel embarrassed.'

'Really, whatever's most comfortable for you.'

She patted his arm, affectionately. 'I like you. So, Thom, what you need to do now is go and see the veg patch – Alistair's out there waiting to give the tour – it's the love of his life. He's very boring about it but you'll humour him, won't you?'

Thom smiled, liking this woman and her soft Welsh accent and her moments of private reverie. Thom heard the bath taps running upstairs, and guessed Susan was going to have a long morning soak in Welsh water, by way of anointment. She said it was her favourite thing to do here.

'Belief, and love,' Lindy said, cryptically. 'Go and take a look.'

He wandered out with his coffee, across a patio, and into an extensive kitchen garden that spread up the hillside. Alistair seemed to be waiting for him by some rambling courgettes, wearing his pair of off-white tennis shorts. 'Come to see my veggies, Thom?' Alistair said in a sing song voice.

'Lead the way.'

Alistair quickly explained how the veg patch was a miracle to have grown at all. 'Acidic water, absolute absence of workable topsoil, rock shale peppering the ground,' he listed. 'And so cold this high up the mountain the spring's a month late. When we came to Blaen,' Alastair explained, stopping by some waist high fennel, 'it was nothing but sheep dung and wiregrass out here.' A gentle Welsh intonation came through in every other word. 'The dung used to get between the toes,' he added. 'Had to flick the stuff off each time I went in the kitchen. So that was no good, no good at all. But then I thought to myself, I did, I thought – *dung*!'

'Dung?'

'Hundreds of years of it. My veggies *love* it. Can't get enough.' He pointed out his crops, proudly, with the tip of his trowel, 'aubergines, peppers, leeks, potatoes, garlic, cabbages, cauliflowers. You see? Up there, Thom, you won't believe but there's espaliers of quince, plum and damsons. Never been grown in this valley, not to my knowledge.' He looked thoroughly amazed at the things he was saying. 'And hot Welsh chillies – who'd have thought it!'

Alistair's tennis shorts were frayed and well worn, and it was clear he wasn't wearing pants under them. The button above the fly was missing, and the shorts seemed to be held up by chance – perhaps by a single tooth of the zip.

'But oh – the slugs – we do have a problem with slugs. Oh yes. They come down from the crags during the night, and feast themselves rotten.'

'My dad drowns them in beer,' Thom said.

'Oh – really?'

Thom realised that to this man, all life was probably sacred. 'You don't kill them, do you?'

Alistair smiled gently and rubbed his chin. 'No, not that. I *negotiate* with them. I persuade them to go different ways. The slug is a fellow of habit, you know, much like you and me. They like to follow their own trails – they get nervous striking out on new paths.'

'Right.'

'So if you wash their trails away, behind them like – you can coax them to slide off into the fields, little by little.'

'That seems quite a lot of effort.'

'But so much *fun*, too!' Alistair replied, enthusiastically. 'Lindy picks them up and takes them down the lane on her bike.'

Thom imagined the mother of his girlfriend riding naked on the old sit up and beg bike he'd seen by the front door, a bucket of slugs hanging from a handlebar.

'Susan is very fond of you,' Alistair said, out of the blue. 'We grew her too in this valley. I don't know how she manages in London, I really don't.'

Thom nodded, not wanting to comment. Seeing Susan here, in this remote part of Wales, was explaining much of her behaviour: her bewilderment to be sitting on a packed London bus, her moments of dreamy withdrawal in noisy situations, the thick jumpers she wore in a flat that was never going to have the coldness of this draughty farmhouse, the desire to walk, always. Seeing this Welsh quietness, the soft green light that fell on the hillsides, the damp stoney smell of . the air, Susan clearly found the rest of the world a compromised place.

'She hasn't always made the right choices,' Alistair added, somewhat mischievously. 'Not with men.' He bent down to tend the vegetables, scratching the soil with his trowel.

Whatever held those shorts up, it was a tension Thom felt very aware of. Surely a bend in the wrong direction, or pulling too hard at a weed, and those shorts would spring open. Nakedness was one thing, but *sudden nakedness*, surely, another. The missing button, the teeth on the old zip about to slip – it seemed Alistair's clothes were itching to come off.

Sure enough, later in the day the shorts were gone. From an upstairs window Thom looked down on Alistair, now completely naked, as he wheeled a barrow up the brick path between the vegetables. Thom was struck by the skinniness of the man's legs, compared to the tight paunch of his belly, his bony barrelled chest and his sloping shoulders, all that skin pink-raw in the cold lunchtime shadow behind the house. And he was strangely hairy in places. For example, above his bum, on either side of his spine, the goat-like beginnings of a satyr's tail.

'Your dad's not wearing any clothes,' he said to Susan, dryly.

'So he approves of you,' she replied, unconcerned.

'Really? So if he likes your boyfriends he takes his clothes off?'

'That's about it.'

Through the window, Alistair began to fork manure over a row of onions. His balls swung freely between his legs. Oh dear, Thom muttered, to himself. The only clothing Alistair wore was a pair of lace-less trainers. It made him look like a cricket pitch streaker.

Thom considered whether Lindy, somewhere in the house, had also removed her clothes. He imagined her lurking in the darkened hallway, wriggling out of that loose dress like she was doing a hula hoop, then hanging it on the peg next to her husband's shorts.

'What about your mum?' he asked. 'Will she be stripped off by now?'

Susan didn't reply. He turned to see her giving him a weary heard-it-all before look.

'Dad usually takes his lead from her.'

'OK. So that elasticated dress will already be hung up?'

'Don't get silly about it,' she said, and he realised she'd probably had this same conversation with all her previous boyfriends. They'd all said the wrong thing in their own way, and they'd all not lasted.

'I'm teasing,' he said.

'Good. I'm going to have a bath.'

'Another one?'

'It's what I do here.'

While she ran the bath, Thom studied the naked man in the garden. Alistair was pulling up vegetables, carefully, diligently, with a curious look of – not quite sadness – but concern, as if he was doing a great wrong. At times, he had to straddle the rows, squatting as he tugged the carrots from the ground, the soil-dirty leaves suddenly springing free and slapping him in the groin.

Thom decided to go downstairs and join him, determined to act more maturely, more casually, than the list of Susan's failed boyfriends. The whole weekend had the aspect of a test. A meet the parents test. He would pass with flying colours.

In the kitchen there was a homely smell of baking coming from the Aga, but no sign of anyone. He tasted some leftover dough from the side of a mixing bowl. Scone mix, he thought, or some sort of Welsh cake. He went outside.

'Hi, Alistair,' he called.

'Hello!' Alistair replied, cheerily, holding up a bunch of carrots in his hand, like a prize. It was an absurd sight, really, a naked man holding aloft a bunch of dirty carrots.

'They look great.'

'We'll have them tonight.' Thom couldn't help noticing the older man's balls retracting, as Alistair laughed. 'Suse in the bath?'

'Yes.'

'She likes a bath.' Alistair bent to the vegetables again, and Thom sat down. Good, that went OK, he thought. It was a proving of sorts, to have had this conversation, however simple. He'd been able to talk, man to naked man, and not be embarrassed about it. He took out a book and began to read, and easily read six or seven sentences before realising he hadn't taken a single word in. Someone was in the kitchen: the Aga's heavy door was being opened. Bowls were being put in the sink. He turned a page, realising he'd been on the same one just a bit too long.

Lindy walked out onto the patio, totally naked, carrying a tray of fresh baked scones. The scones, it appeared, might have been a subtle way of concealing herself, distracting him. But for Thom the tray of scones made it worse. This woman, the mother of his girlfriend, her nudity and the fresh warm scones seemed to be a combined offer.

'I've been busy,' she said. She put the tray down on the patio table and stood before him.

Resolutely, heroically, he looked her in the eye.

'Good,' she said. 'So – what will you have?'

Altogether, what needed to be accepted and what needed to be declined seemed catastrophically mingled. At the edge of his vision, her large weighty breasts looked back at him. Two sad unblinking eyes.

'They – they all look delicious, Mrs Maddox.'

'Oh, please, it's *Lindy*,' she said. 'Susan!' she called, to the open window above them: 'Scones.'

'She's having a bath,' he said.

'Again? That girl!' Lindy started to walk back to the kitchen, the crease beneath her wide dimpled arse making a splendid smile for him and for him alone.

This was a bizarre moment, Thom considered, congratulating himself that he hadn't giggled or blushed or done anything immature. But it was still bizarre. The parents had just taken their clothes off. And no one was mentioning it.

From the kitchen he began to hear Lindy singing a little made up song. He couldn't make out all the words, but it seemed to be about the wind turbine that Alistair had tried, and failed, to make. Prompted by their talk, earlier. Then a second verse about some sort of home-made garden shower. It was a charming song.

'We have ravens here,' Lindy said when she returned, carrying small ceramic pots of jam and cream. 'They circle above the crags and drop stones on the rabbits. They're very clever birds and have a tremendous aim.'

He looked up at the crags, wishing briefly that he was up there, a free and uncomplicated space.

'Now,' Lindy said, cutting open one of the scones. 'Are you a jam on top or a cream on top man?'

He'd finished a second scone before Susan came out. She walked languidly across the patio, kissed him on the cheek, and lay a hand on his shoulder. Susan was taller in Wales. Her joints relaxed.

'You all getting on?' she said, good humoured.

Her mother beamed at her. 'He's sweet, Sue. Where did you find this lovely man?'

Susan kissed him again, sealing the general approval. She reached for a scone. 'I thought I could take the car, Mum, and show him Crickhowell. Would you mind?'

'What's in Crickhowell?' he asked.

'Nothing, but it's not here and I'm sure you need a break from my parents.'

'There's a farmers' market,' Lindy said.

'Right. There you go. There's a farmers' market.' Susan ate the scone, holding her hand under it to catch the crumbs. Thom noticed her wrist resembled her mother's. Thicker than it should be. It was another of several similarities between these two women he'd noticed. The way they sat, for example, with the right foot placed neatly in front of the left. A slight lumpiness to the knees, as if they shared an extra bone there. Lindy looked back at him, trying to guess his thoughts. Sitting here, he realised, was a naked version of his girlfriend, given thirty years.

In Crickhowell they found an impressive cheese stall in the corner of the square that stood for the farmers' market, but every other shop in the town seemed to be Poundland, or a version of it. They walked up the high street, turned, and walked down it again.

'Pub?' he suggested.

'Thought you'd never ask.'

They found a pub and sat at the window. He had a pint of some locally brewed beer, and she decided to have a cappuccino from a machine they had to switch on for her.

'Well, here we are. Here's my home,' she said.

'Cheers,' he replied, raising his drink. Through the window he looked up the high street. It had started to drizzle and the few people out there – who were mostly old – seemed to bend into the weather. They looked grim faced. Crickhowell looked a grumpy sort of place. Having spent the morning with a couple of naturists – who radiated a sense of enthusiasm – it suddenly appeared that it might be the drab coloured fleeces, the shapeless anoraks, the ill-fitting jeans, that might be making these people in Crickhowell so heavy and depressed. He compared them to the nimble way Alistair tiptoed through the veg patch, or Lindy's easy jolly swagger as she carried the scones.

'I'm having odd thoughts,' he said.

She laughed. 'How are you finding it at Blaen-y-cym? Is it OK?'

'Fine.'

'And the general nudiness?'

'Totally cool. It didn't really occur to me,' he lied.

She sipped her coffee. They had these silences, often, like he was expected to keep the conversations going. She looked through the window.

'What about you?' he asked. 'How's it being at home?'

She shrugged, non-committal. 'Mum and Dad wind me up – you know that.'

He nodded, half-remembering old conversations, but not quite getting what her angle had been.

'It's all the lovey-dovey stuff,' she explained. 'It's cringing.' She described how her father left snowdrops or bluebells at her mum's breakfast placemat, without fail, after the walks he took at dawn. Later in the year it would be dandelions, an owl's pellet, lichen, even moss. He'd lay them out for her, making a gift out of something he found simply beautiful.

'He does that?'

'Every day.'

Thom suspected a comparison might be being made. Him, rushed each morning, standing up to eat his toast, no time for wandering around hills filling his pockets with trinkets, thinking of beauty. He decided to draw attention to it:

'I'm sorry, for not doing that.'

'Doing what?'

'Leaving you little daily gifts.'

'We have jobs, Thom.'

'Still.'

'If you did that for me – I'd find it weird. No one does that, at our age.'

'It's sweet. Isn't it?'

She clearly didn't think so. 'The way they behave – it's like the honeymoon never wore off.'

'So what about your mum – what does she do for him?'

She smiled, despite herself. 'Mum makes vegetable sculptures for the dinner table – she does these little comic still lives with them – you know – aubergine men with carrot legs and mushroom caps, stuck together with cocktail sticks, playing courgette saxophones. There was this entire Mardi Gras band, once. It was amazing.'

'Wow.'

'She sings, too.'

'Yeah – I heard one this morning. About one of your father's inventions.'

'The one about the wind turbine?'

'Yeah. For what it's worth – I think your parents are great,' he said. 'You know – it's clear they're still really in love.' He'd been struck by it, the abundance of affection they had for each other, mentally comparing them to his own parents, who were always scoring points in petty arguments against one another. A thirty year war with no achievable goals, no conceivable end.

'Don't be fooled by it – it's not always like that,' she said. 'They can get pretty bitter.'

Like us, he thought. No. Bitterness wasn't the issue – it was a general distance he felt. Somehow they never became close enough, they never stopped and just held each other. They were always too busy. All they needed to do was appreciate what they had and be more meaningful with their time. Let the world turn without them.

Back at Blaen-y-cym, in the early evening light, he climbed up to the crags behind the house. The sheep eyed him suspiciously as he passed, standing a few feet away and making little stumbling runs to keep their distance. They seemed so nervous, he couldn't believe any one of them had ever walked into the farmhouse kitchen and jumped on the table. Maybe Lindy had been joking, or making some kind of point he couldn't work out. When he stopped he listened to the sound of the sheep chewing, and the noises from the valley rising up at him. Streams, running through the bracken, somewhere along the hill. There were bones among the rocks, lots of them. Perhaps they were from rabbits, where the ravens had pelted them.

Blaen-y-cym looked peaceful. A peaceful place to grow up in, and to grow old in, but a place Susan couldn't wait to get away from after a few days, or so she claimed. She was having yet another bath. That was the third of the day. In London, she showered, but in Wales she seemed to spend as much time as possible soaking. The gentle Welsh water, she explained, opened her pores and softened her bones. As if she was porous here, whereas in London the hard water ran straight off, never quite cleansing her.

He watched Lindy and Alistair come out of a side door, carrying what seemed like a single divan bed. They were doing up the spare room, so it made sense. Both of them were naked, and they carried the bed to one of the sheds, where there was some other furniture waiting to be recycled.

They walked gingerly, both in their laceless trainers, making little adjustments with their grip. It looked like a scene in a comedy sketch: a couple of randy lovers, caught mid-act, having to carry their bed around.

Back at the farmhouse, he walked into the en-suite to find Susan was still in the bath. She lay perfectly still while he sat on a stool next to her. He dipped the ends of his fingers in the water.

'Hello, you,' she said. 'How was the climb?'

'Lovely. You come from a beautiful place.'

He pictured their life in London, constantly fuelled by their jobs, their social lives, their endless day-to-day struggle to convince themselves they were going in the right direction. They never stopped. Here, they were in the stillness of her family home, a farmhouse in a valley that hardly stirred, it had exposed a silence they didn't know quite how to fill.

He thought about getting in with her, but knew she didn't like sharing baths. Bathing was a special thing for her, and sharing was somehow smutty, a transgression, even if it wasn't. Plus the bath was quite narrow. They'd have to negotiate with their legs and it just wouldn't work. Not with her.

He smiled, looking at her knees again. He'd never particularly noticed them in London, but here, half submerged, reminding him of her mother, they seemed peculiar.

'What are you looking at?'

'Your knees.'

She dipped them in the water and then let them rise again. He watched the water drying on her skin.

'Have you seen Mum and Dad?' she asked.

'They're carrying a bed round the garden.'

'Really?'

He thought about telling her what a strange sight it had been, the two of them, naked, carrying the bed, but felt unsure how critical she allowed him to be when he talked about her parents. There were mixed signals. She found them maddening, had regular spats with her mother in particular, but then there'd been that extended hug in the entrance hall. A complex loyalty.

'So – have you never been tempted – to join in with the naturist stuff?' he asked.

'No.' She sounded perplexed, as if he was a million miles away from understanding this thing. 'There've been occasions, Thom. Some of my school friends did it.'

'What – with your parents?'

'Yeah.'

'What happened?'

'I'm getting out, Thom, it's getting cold.'

Dinner was an oddly formal affair. They sat in a chilly room around a long dark table and ate off fine china plates with silver cutlery. Lindy wore her elasticated tent-dress. Clearly there was a more complicated set of rules about nudity that Thom didn't quite understand. Perhaps dressing for dinner was something even a naturist couldn't give up on. In the centre of the table were two of Lindy's vegetable sculptures: a couple of standard poodles, one made of cauliflower florets, and the other made from broccoli. The starter was purple kale, dressed with lemon and thyme. After that, they ate new potatoes with butter and chives, leeks, and some of those dark red carrots, washed and steamed and served whole. It was difficult to avoid the image of Alistair squatting over the carrot bed, tugging at the plants while his genitals shook and brushed the leaves. They drank a syrupy and deceptively strong parsnip wine, and by the time dessert was served, Thom felt unable to trust his judgement. He looked at his plate of steamed rhubarb with honey and oatmeal, wondering whether it was the wine that was making him feel at a remove from what was going on in the dining room, as if he was watching himself act in a play. The cauliflower poodle stared at him, eerily.

When Lindy went to fetch cream from the kitchen, a piece of her dress became wedged between her bum cheeks. It looked, momentarily, like her bum was trying to take a bite from the material and, for the first time, Thom wondered whether he preferred his girlfriend's mother without her clothes on. Naked, she could be seen at face value, but with the silly dress on, there was an issue of poor concealment that drew attention to her body. The dress made her *more* naked, he thought.

He decided to down his wine, thinking a level of drunkenness was probably the best approach.

After the meal, they retired to the snug – a red walled room with three sofas in it and a woodburner set into a large hearth. Thom sat next to Susan, feeling the meal had been a success and that Susan must be thinking along similar lines by the way she curled herself into him. Just the night to go, and tomorrow they'd be setting off in the car, returning to London. He'd be back on home turf.

Lindy came in, bringing candles from the dining table to put on the mantelpiece and, standing on the rug in the centre of the room, she wriggled out of her tent-dress. She let it drop onto the floor and then she kicked it onto the chair with a toe.

Alistair followed suit. He slipped his tennis shorts off and folded them onto the armrest of the sofa, letting out a satisfied sigh as he did so. Susan didn't seem to notice the parental striptease. Again, Thom had the sense that this moment was another of the pre-arranged tests in some kind of Maddox-family challenge; one he could easily fail. He chose to meet it head on, to show his lack of fear:

'I think it's great – being like you are,' he said, trying not to sound like he was calling them freaks. 'I mean the naturism.'

'You do?' Lindy said, obviously pleased.

'Sure. It's brilliant.' He noticed the wine had affected his voice. He made a mental note to speak carefully.

'We used to wear clothes before Suse was born,' Lindy said. 'All through the seventies – when everyone else was taking *off* their clothes – we were...'

'...buttoned up,' Alistair said, with a wink.

'Yes. Buttoned up. Looking back – I don't really understand it. Do you, love? Why were we so stiff back then?'

Alistair shrugged, happily. 'I think it takes time in a marriage, until you're so familiar with the other person that you hardly notice whether they're wearing clothes or not. I mean – I really can't tell, nowadays.'

'And it saves a lot of money,' Lindy said, with a conspiratorial whisper, 'not to be following the fashions.'

'Like you ever did, Mum,' Susan said.

'In my time, darling, I was able to turn a head or two.'

'So who went first?' Thom asked. 'I mean – was it something you both agreed on, or what?' Susan gave him a little warning glance, as if to say there's more to my parents than their nudity. Change the subject.

'Me,' Alistair said, his eyes sparkling in the candlelight. 'Soon after Suse came along in fact. I saw this beautiful baby – and you were, Susan, you were a wonder – and you're there – this perfect little warm-skinned baby, and I said to myself: Alistair, how did you get to be so far away from *that*?'

'He said he was going to take his clothes off for an entire week,' Lindy continued, affectionately, 'and I told him – you do that for a whole week and then I'll join you.'

Susan tapped Thom on his arm: 'You do realise I've heard this story a thousand times.'

Thom looked at Susan's parents as they smiled in the candlelight. It wasn't their nudity that bothered him. It was how at ease they were. It was rare to meet two people so devoted, who seemed to wake up each day so full of love and contentment. It was as if the Welsh mountain air breathed a spell on them, each night. Perhaps this valley really was a magical place. A place of healing. Their two hearts beating as one, and a daily goal to do nothing but appreciate each other. Maybe it was the clothes, after all, that might be keeping him and Susan apart? Maybe putting on clothes made them look and act like other people. Made them disguised.

He felt he needed to tell Alistair and Lindy that in just twenty-four hours their relationship had made a profound impact on him. Alistair smiled at him, as if reading his thoughts. Thom felt such warmth in there, in the snug, with the red walls and the feel of the parsnip wine in him.

'I must admit,' he began, 'before I came here I was a little nervous – I'm from – you know, a fairly conventional background. But you've really opened my eyes to all this.'

'That's good, Thom,' Alistair said, 'that's good to hear.'

'In fact –' he stopped himself, enjoying the sense of a decision, carefully poised. 'Actually – would it be crazy, I mean – you've got to say if it is – but how crazy would it be if I took my clothes off?'

Lindy laughed. 'What, now?'

'Yeah.'

'Too much wine, methinks?' Susan said, visibly tight-lipped.

'No – no – come on,' Thom said. 'I'm serious.'

Susan went stern. 'Why would you do that, Thom?' she asked, somewhere between a smile and something else that wasn't quite formed.

Thom looked back at her, wondering why she was being so brittle about this. He realised there was a problem here, a problem between them two – where there was this kind of repressed thinking. It had grown up in all sorts of areas between them. Not spending enough time on each other, not laughing enough. Not having as much fun as they should, because somehow over the months, their default state was to self-police against spontaneity. They were trying to act out some kind of couple he knew he didn't – deep down – belong in. They were making this constant show to be mature and grown up and in fact they were just – *boring*.

'Right,' he said, feeling angry about all sorts of slights he'd built up. All sorts of vague resentments about the couple they'd become. He unbuttoned his shirt and took it off.

'You're going to drop your trousers now, aren't you, Thom,' Susan said, sounding like a bossy teacher. *Some of my school friends used to do it*, she'd actually said that, up in the bedroom. They'd taken their clothes off to join in with the parents. So why was it all OK then and not OK now? Perhaps, he wanted to tell her, perhaps if you and I were a little more free-spirited like your parents, then perhaps we'd get along better.

He had his hand on his belt. The decision already made. He was beyond the point of going back. Taking his trousers and pants off was just a formality now. He stood, unbuttoned his jeans, and pulled them and his boxers down, in one go.

Quickly. Disastrously. Even before he'd stepped out of his jeans he knew what a terrible mistake this was. He stood, exposing himself, looking down at his terrified penis and the sight of his cast off pants.

'Well done, lad,' Alistair said, in a room that suddenly felt incredibly silent. 'How do you feel?'

'Good,' Thom said, lying. He felt appalled.

He glanced at Lindy, nervously, wanting an ally at least, and saw that she was openly checking him out. Unashamedly, she was appraising his groin. He sat down on the sofa as quick as he could. How dare she, he thought. All day long he'd assiduously *not* looked at her, and yet here she was, a seasoned pro, been doing it for years, and eyeing him up like a teenager.

'I can't believe you've just done that,' Susan said, quietly, shielding her face with a hand. She was trying to sound amused, that this twist in the evening might yet be made into a joke, but he knew from the tone of her voice there were so many other layers to it, so many other things she was going to say. On the phone to a friend – *So he stood there, right in front of Mum and Dad, and pulled his pants off.* It just couldn't be said in any other way. Or to him – *You showed absolutely no respect for them, did you?*

The atmosphere in the room had entirely changed. He lay his hands on his lap, a desperate concealment, attempting to talk about tomorrow, what they might do before the journey back, but it seemed ridiculous now. Everything he said was ridiculous.

He stared at the pathetic pile of his clothes where they lay on the rug, wishing his boxers weren't left so openly displayed.

Lindy spoke quietly and deliberately: 'You're nicely built, Thom.'

'Mum!' Susan said, harshly.

'I do a lot of running,' Thom said, hearing his voice as if it was coming from another room. Running was something he'd like to be doing, right now, as fast as he could.

Lindy continued, addressing her husband. 'You could do with a little more exercise yourself, Alistair.'

'I'm quite happy the shape I am, love.'

But Lindy hadn't quite finished. She looked at her husband with a sense of sadness, that there was an element of long-standing disappointment between them.

'You've let yourself go – on the tummy, for one.'

Alistair stood. He proudly smacked his belly. 'That,' he said, 'is the shape of a man who is content.'

Lindy raised her eyebrows, as if there was more to be said.

'Anyway –' Alistair started, with a slightly ugly sneer. Thom could see the man was highly vexed. 'Anyway – what about you...' he gestured towards his wife, at her wide thighs filling the armchair, her belly hanging in a sad bow over the wisps of pubic hair. With a wave of his hand he drew attention to it, to a general sense of disgust.

'Mum, Dad!' Susan said. 'Don't.'

Alistair stood angrily, holding back the words he knew he could say. Instead, his chest blushed pink, and his cock pointed like a crooked finger towards his wife, accusing her. Lindy got up and stormed out of the room.

Alone with Susan in her bedroom, she was so furious, so full of all the things she was trying to formulate, that she actually said nothing. Eventually, lying stiffly in bed next to him, with the light off, she managed: 'I can't believe you did that.'

Here goes, Thom thought.

'Have you got nothing to say?'

'I thought it was the thing to do – I thought you said your school friends used to do it?'

'Once. For a stupid dare. It was embarrassing then – and now...' She didn't finish the sentence.

Thom realised this was probably the beginning of a whole series of talks they might have, possibly the beginning of an end for them, too. He'd made a fool of himself. He'd made a spectacle. But hadn't his intentions been good ones – hadn't he been so full of admiration for the parents' abundance of love for each other that he wanted to try and discover it with Susan? Unfortunately, exposing himself had exposed them both, and their limitations.

Unable to sleep, and suspecting Susan was lying there, fuming, waiting for an argument neither of them wanted, he got out of bed and wandered through the unlit farmhouse.

In the dining room, both the vegetable poodles had lost their heads. He stood for a while in the snug, trying to replay the exact sequence of events. The parental striptease, his rash decision to join in, Lindy's libidinous look, and Alistair's reaction. Whichever way he viewed it, it looked bad. With a sigh he went through the darkened kitchen and out onto the patio. He walked up through the veg patch, where he noticed several huge slugs, very black, very long, were sliding towards the courgettes. Behind the outbuilding he found the bed the parents had brought out. The mattress was damp with dew, but he sat on it regardless. There were sheep around him, low down on the hillside. He watched a couple of them cautiously crossing the patio, and one, nervously step into the kitchen where he'd left the door open. He looked up to Susan's window, wondering what the morning would bring him, and whether he would ever come to this place again. The source of the river, he thought, abstractly.

From inside the kitchen, he heard the sheep, jumping onto the table.

About the Authors

Jonathan Buckley studied English Literature at Sussex University, where he stayed on to take an MA. From there he moved to King's College, London, where he researched the work of the Scottish poet/artist Ian Hamilton Finlay. After working as a university tutor, stage hand, maker of theatrical sets and props, bookshop manager, decorator and builder, he was commissioned in 1987 to write *The Rough Guide to Venice & the Veneto*. He went on to become an editorial director at Rough Guides, and to write further guidebooks on Tuscany & Umbria and Florence, as well as contributing to *The Rough Guide to Classical Music* and *The Rough Guide to Opera*. His first novel, *The Biography of Thomas Lang*, was published by Fourth Estate in 1997. It was followed by *Xerxes* (1999), *Ghost MacIndoe* (2001), *Invisible* (2004), *So He Takes the Dog* (2006), *Contact* (2010), *Telescope* (2011), *Nostalgia* (2013) and *The river is the river* (2015).

From 2003 to 2005 he held a Royal Literary Fund fellowship at the University of Sussex, and from 2007 to 2011 was an Advisory Fellow of the Royal Literary Fund. He also works as a freelance non-fiction editor.

Mark Haddon's first novel for adults was the prize-winning *The Curious Incident of the Dog in the Night-Time* (2003), which was later adapted by Simon Stephens into a prize-winning play. His subsequent novels are *A Spot of Bother* (2006) and *The Red House* (2012). Mark has written for TV and radio and published a collection of poetry, *The Talking Horse, the Sad Girl and the Village Under the Sea*. His play, *Polar Bears*, was produced at the Donmar in 2010. His short story 'The Gun' was short listed for the Sunday Times EFG Short Story Award and the O'Henry Prize. *The Pier Falls*, a collection of his short stories, will be published by Cape in May 2016.

Frances Leviston was born in Edinburgh in 1982 and grew up in Sheffield. She read English at St Hilda's College, Oxford, and has an MA in Writing from Sheffield Hallam University. *Public Dream*, her first collection of poetry, was published in 2007 by Picador and shortlisted for the T. S. Eliot Prize. Her second collection, *Disinformation*, appeared from Picador in 2015. She lives in Durham.

Hilary Mantel grew up in the Peak District in Derbyshire and was educated at a Cheshire convent school, the LSE and Sheffield University, graduating in law in 1973. She was subsequently a teacher and a social worker, living for 9 years in Africa and the Middle East. She became a full-time writer in the mid 1980s, and is the author of eleven novels, two short story collections and a memoir, *Giving Up The Ghost*. She writes both historical and contemporary fiction and her settings range from a South African township under apartheid to Paris in the Revolution, from a city in twentieth century Saudi Arabia to rural Ireland in the eighteenth century. Her novel *Wolf Hall* is about Thomas Cromwell, chief minister to Henry VIII. It won the 2009 Man Booker prize, the inaugural Walter Scott prize, and in the US won the National Book Critics Circle Award. Her second Cromwell novel, *Bring Up The Bodies*, won the 2012 Man Booker Prize and the Costa 'Book of the Year' Award. Both novels were adapted for television, and she worked with the adapter Mike Poulton on a stage version which was performed in Stratford-upon-Avon, the West End and Broadway. She is a Governor of The Royal Shakespeare Company. In 2014, she published a book of short stories *The Assassination of Margaret Thatcher*. She is currently working on the final novel of the Thomas Cromwell trilogy *The Mirror & The Light*. Hilary Mantel was appointed DBE in 2014. She lives with her husband in East Devon.

Jeremy Page grew up on the North Norfolk coast. His first novel, *Salt*, (Penguin, 2007) was shortlisted for the Commonwealth Writers' Prize for 'Best First Book' and the Jelf First Novel Award. His second novel, *The Wake* (Penguin, 2009), won the fiction prize at the East Anglian Book Awards, and was shortlisted for the New Angle Prize. *The Collector of Lost Things* (Little Brown, 2013) was longlisted for the Dublin Imac Prize. He is also a scriptwriter and script editor for various UK film and TV companies, a journalist, and has taught Creative Writing at the UEA as well as tutoring and mentoring for various universities and at the London Film School. He lives in London and is married with three children.

About the Award

THE BBC NATIONAL SHORT STORY AWARD with Book Trust is one of the most prestigious prizes for a single short story and celebrates the best in home-grown short fiction. The ambition of the Award, which is now in its tenth year, is to expand opportunities for British writers, readers and publishers of the short story. The winning author receives £15,000, the runner-up £3,000 and the three further shortlisted authors £500 each. All five shortlisted stories are broadcast on BBC Radio 4.

The previous winners are: Lionel Shriver (2014), Sarah Hall (2013), Miroslav Penkov (in 2012, when the Award accepted international entries to commemorate the Olympics); D. W. Wilson (2011); David Constantine (2010); Kate Clanchy (2009); Clare Wigfall (2008); Julian Gough (2007) and James Lasdun (2006).

Award Partners:

> BBC RADIO 4 is the world's single biggest commissioner of short stories. Short stories are broadcast every week attracting more than a million listeners.
> www.bbc.co.uk/radio4

> Book Trust is Britain's largest reading charity. It has a vision of a society where nobody misses out on the life-changing benefits that reading can bring. Book Trust is responsible for a number of successful national reading promotions, sponsored book prizes and creative reading projects aimed at encouraging readers to discover and enjoy books. www.booktrust.org.uk

More on: www.booktrust.org.uk/bbcnssa
Follow us on Twitter: @Booktrust #BBCNSSA